# A PATIENT ENEMY

Published by Tigress Publishing

Copyright 2010 Kelley Theron

ISBN-13: 978-0-9801510-6-0
ISBN-10: 0-9801510-
Library of Congress Control Number: 2009942270
Printed in the United States of America
Editor: Amelia Boldaji
Design: Steve Montiglio
Cover Photo: Steve Montiglio

Requests for such permission should be submitted to:
Tigress Publishing
4742 42nd Avenue SW #551
Seattle, Washington 98116-4553

This is a work of fiction. All names, characters and incidents either are the product of the author's imagination or are used ficticiously. Any resemblance to actual persons, living or dead, business establishments, other events or locales is entirely coincidental.

*For my husband, for always believing I can do anything I dare attempt, and for being oblivious to my faults, or maybe just pretending to be and loving me in spite of them.*

*And to my amazing children, the two biggest pieces of my heart, who remain fearless even though they are better educated than most about the dangers of the world, and who have always been proud of me even though I'm not like other moms. Thanks for understanding that I can't stop myself from finishing that repetitive warning for you to be careful, because I don't have a spare in the closet, and you are truly irreplaceable. You are my joy!*

*And for the hundreds of victims of violent crimes whom I've had the privilege of meeting over the years - You do the bravest thing of all when you gather your strength and decide to tell the truth about what happened to you - and then repeat it all again inside a courtroom. You testify in the presence of the person who hurt you in the hopes that justice will be served. I am in awe of your courage.*

didn't recognize the dream as a premonition, and maybe it wasn't. At the time it seemed unusual, but not upsetting. In fact, although I remembered the dream when I woke up, I didn't attribute it any significance until later. Sometimes even now I wonder whether it was a warning I could have heeded, a chance offered by fate that I didn't recognize in time.

The dream was about the night of my eighth grade dance. I was fourteen and desperately trying to rise above my average looks and figure, and look glamorous and beautiful. I realize now that I looked very pretty in my light blue dress. At the time though, I had the fear of looking less than perfect. Perfect hair, perfect make-up, perfect shoes and purse, to go with a beautiful dress. It was all that mattered.

I was never a moody girl, but there were times when I wished I was beautiful, really beautiful, like the girls on the cover of Seventeen magazine. I was cute, and some said pretty, but at times it wasn't quite enough. More

1

importantly (I know now, but didn't then), I was a good girl, reliable and smart: Kate, the A-student who respected her parents and teachers and made good choices. I was middle-of-the-road popular at school with a group of cherished friends, not someone who was teased or ostracized, but also not quite on that fast-track train to high school popularity that the beautiful blonde cheerleader girls had boarded. Still, I had good friends, and I was happy. The only time I felt insecure and possibly lacking, was in situations when my physical appearance (please, God – beauty?) was at the forefront – something to be noticed and critiqued.

I'm explaining all this so that you won't think me some kind of monster for how I treated Mia that night.

I loved Mia with all my heart. She was ten years younger than I, and at four years old had our whole family wrapped around her pre-schooler's finger. We lived on Walnut Avenue in Middleton, Washington in a sensible brick three bedroom, one bathroom home with our mother Dorothy, and father. Our older brother, Robert, was nineteen years old and in the Army overseas. My mother, who was forty-one when she found out (surprise!) that she was pregnant with Mia, cried on and off for three days. My father, then forty-five, kept saying, "It's not that bad," while forcing a smile that belied his disappointment that they would soon be returning to the land of diapers and nighttime feedings.

I, on the other hand, at the age of nine (ten by the time Mia was born) was thrilled at the thought of a baby in the house.

When Mia arrived, she did more than compensate for the shock of her conception. She was the most beautiful baby anyone had ever seen. I know that because I heard nurses, neighbors, and numerous aunts and cousins proclaim that was true, over and over. I had to agree that they were right.

My dad had black hair and strong masculine features, and my mother was a petite, light brown haired beauty. My brother Robert had inherited my father's coloring and good looks, and I had inherited enough of a mix from my parents that I could be described as pretty. Mia, who was born "baby girl Hunt," had a striking full head of auburn hair, and depending on who was talking, either the face of an angel, or a movie star. Her features were petite, like our mother's, but our father's face was in there too, blending with our mother's features into perfection.

Mom, who knew, but would never admit that she was a beauty in her own right, realized that her youngest child would surpass her in the looks department. Although she had planned on the sensible name of Susan for a girl, or Michael for a boy, Mom took one look at the new baby and changed her mind. She was named Mia in the end, a name that sounded exotic and movie-star special to my mother.

I have to admit, even as a child I was slightly jealous of Mia's looks, and to a lesser degree, her name. I say to a lesser degree because the name Mia did fit her, and Kate fit me. More than that, it was hard to be jealous of Mia in any kind of mean-spirited, truly envious way because I loved her so much, and I was proud that she was my sister. The dream brought all that back. In the dream I was dressed in my lovely blue dress and almost ready to go to the dance. Mia had been skirting around and making a pest of herself, as four-year-olds will do. Think of a small dog running in circles around a horse. I tolerated it because I knew that Mia adored me and was fascinated by watching me get ready. I was normally a jeans and t-shirt kind of girl, and to her (and to the rest of the student body at Jefferson Junior High School, or so I hoped) this was a magical transformation.

I stood in front of the mirror, admiring my look. I was pretty pleased with my general appearance. My shoulder-length brown hair was in a fancy up-do, courtesy of my mom, who copied it from a magazine. The dress was form-fitting in the bust and waist, and loose and flowing in the skirt, which ended just below my knees. I can still remember the swish-swish of it against my legs. Mom had bought a pair of those dye-able white pumps that had been dyed to match the same light blue of the dress. (I also remember the little pinch of the shoes at my heel, and wondering how grown-ups wore these things every day!) I looked better than I ever had, and I felt like a princess.

As I stood looking in the mirror, Mia continued to circle me. "Katie, Katie, Katie!" She was beside herself with excitement, and although I often thought she was a bit of a bother, I was feeling happy and beautiful. Tolerating her felt easy.

Mia suddenly ran from my room and down the hall. As I added a bit more blue eye shadow, Mia burst back into the room.

"Katie, Katie, Katie, Katie!" she yelled. "WHAT!" I snapped back, with a little more exasperation than I would have liked. The relief of having my "look" turn out well was now subsiding and I was starting to get nervous. The boy I liked, Matthew Zimmer, who knew I existed but had shown no signs of interest, was going to be at the dance of course. Would Matt like how I looked? Would he ask me to dance? What if it was a slow dance? Or what if he didn't even talk to me? And what if he did talk to me, and I said something stupid? My confidence was ebbing and the butterflies were moving in.

"Look, look, I have a surprise for you! Look, look!" Mia continued without noticing my tone.

She opened her outstretched hand to reveal her prize. It was her Tinkerbelle necklace, won from a gumball machine at the local pizza joint. The setting was star-shaped around an image of Tinkerbelle, wand in hand, hovering in the air. It was a typical, twenty-five cent gumball necklace supported on a cheap metal chain. Mia had gotten it about a month ago when Dad gave her a quarter for the machine during a Friday night excursion to the Pizza Palace, and it was her prized possession. So prized, in fact, that she kept it next to her bed, and insisted on kissing Tinkerbelle good night, every night. She usually kissed it good morning, too, and often took it into the bathtub with her. "Tink needs a bath, too!" she explained happily.

"Katie, Katie, wear Tinkerbelle!" she shouted. You'll be the prettiest girl at the dance! No one else will have a necklace like this!" Mia was bubbling over with excitement. She was jumping up and down, thrilled with herself for thinking of such a wonderful idea to make me the belle of the ball.

Even at the time, I recognized what a grand gesture she was making, but I couldn't wear that baby necklace with my beautiful outfit! I know now that I should have put it on and thanked her, and maybe taken it off later, but at the time, I opted for honesty. I know now, that no matter what you've been told, honesty is NOT always the best policy.

"Mia, baby, that's so nice of you. But that necklace is for four-year-olds, not fourteen-year-olds. It would ruin my outfit." I intended to say it nicely, but my tone came out sounding condescending and gruff.

As soon as I'd said the words, I knew they were wrong, but it was too late. Mia stood there and appeared to crumble before me. Tears welled, and then ran down her cheeks. Then I made it worse. I have no excuse. I remember feeling terrible for making her cry, but another part of me was angry that she was making me feel guilty and ruining my moment. "Mia, quit being a baby!" I yelled at her. "Take your stupid necklace and put it back in your room! Mom! Make her leave me alone!" I added for good measure. Mia ran down the hall, crying so hard that she was gasping for air. I heard her throw herself on her bed and sob as if the world was ending.

Mom yelled, "Coming," slightly short of breath as she climbed the stairs. When she got to my door, she gave me a look that was hard to identify. I could see her initial pleasure at my appearance, just as she heard the sobs coming from Mia's room. The pride in her face mixed with sadness, and I started to feel worse. I knew Mom would find out shortly that I was the cause of Mia's tears. I knew I looked beautiful, or at least better than I ever had, but I felt very ugly just then.

After checking on Mia, my wonderful mom, who could always fix anything, came in and gently chastised me. "Kate, she's just a little girl and you're the older sister. I know it's a big night for you, but you should always remember that Mia's the only sister you've got. You've got to watch out for her. She idolizes you, you know." I was ashamed, and I knew Mom could see it. Mom gave me a hug, told me that Mia would get over it, and that I shouldn't let this put a damper on my night. "Besides, you look so pretty, honey! Let me get the camera!"

I went to see Mia in her room before I left. I apologized, and promised her I would come and wake her up when I got home to tell her all about the dance. Before I left, Mia made me kiss Tinkerbelle goodbye and promise that I really loved her little fairy friend. Mia's main concern was that Tinkerbelle's feelings were hurt. After the kiss and promise, all was forgiven. But I never quite forgot the look on Mia's small face just minutes earlier, tears welling over, as she closed her fingers tight around the Tinkerbelle necklace, and yanked it back to clutch it safely against her throat. I don't usually dream about my childhood, so the dream about that night left me feeling nostalgic. I knew it was a dream while I was having it, and was surprised that I could remember the incident with such clarity. I remembered the rustle of my dress as I walked down the stairs, and the cold metal of Tinkerbelle's face as I kissed her (it?) goodbye. I woke up thinking about my family and my childhood and how much I loved my baby sister. I laughed at myself for a second, because I recognized that I still felt the stab of guilt for the harsh way I had spoken to Mia that night. "Wow," I thought, smiling. "No escaping the sins of our childhood!"

My dreams had always been like that – memories, rather than fantasies. It was almost as though I had a photographic memory that could only be viewed in its totality as a dream. While asleep I was able to re-examine what I had lived through at my leisure. It was as if the moment was captured on video. I might dream of Family Fun Night at the carnival and see, as if for the first time, the infinite details that had escaped my notice while awake. This second chance – a reliving of events, really – allowed me to remember things that I hadn't realized I'd even seen. I might notice the wording on a sign that had simply been background before, or recognize and identify that kid eating popcorn in line behind me as the box-boy at the local market, whereas before he had simply looked familiar. And if I took an interest in something I was dreamembering – my word for it – I could slow down and really examine it. I was definitely in charge of what interested me within the memory. As a child I thought that everyone dreamed that way. I spent a brief amount of time at the age of thirteen wondering if something was wrong with me when I found out otherwise, but ended up deciding that the people flying through the clouds at night in their sleep were more likely than I to be the crazy ones.

I savored the memory of my sister's sweetness for a moment, and then I went to get my coffee and fell into my morning routine. I forgot all about the dream until twelve days later, when the call came that changed everything.

met my husband Brett when I was twenty-three and fresh out of college. I had returned to Middleton, Washington, where I grew up and I went into the store where Brett worked at the time, looking for an entry level job. He was on his way out to Starbucks for his break when I picked up the application, and I ended up walking over there with him. I filled out the paperwork while we sat there drinking coffee. A week later, Brett ended up calling to tell me they didn't anticipate hiring anyone for at least a year. Then he asked me out, and as they say, the rest is history. We've lived in the same three bedroom, two bath house in a suburb of Middleton for seven years. Middleton doesn't really need a suburb, as it's only a town of about 85,000 people. But the houses were cheaper on the outskirts, and that was definitely a good reason to drive an extra twenty minutes to work. Besides, after our daughter Kara was born, we knew it was the best place for us to raise a family. And it was. Until the day I got the call about Mia.

April twenty-third was a normal day before I got the call from Mom's neighbor Becky Thompson. Dad passed away two years earlier and Becky had been good about watching out for Mom since then, especially since our brother Robert lives in Illinois with his family. Becky had a heart of gold, but she was the epitome of the "nosy neighbor," a fact that was comforting to me with Mom alone in the house. No suspicious character could get past the end of the block without Becky's notice.

Still Mom lived in a good neighborhood in the house I grew up in, and Becky's calls were far and few between. Occasionally the police would conduct a traffic stop on a car that didn't belong in the neighborhood, or a door-to-door salesman would seem suspicious, and Becky would assume they were in for a rash of burglaries. She usually called me "just to let you know" that there had been some suspicious characters around, in case I wanted to check on Mom. Brett called Becky a busy-body, and she was, but her heart was in the right place. Between motherhood and working as the office manager for a pediatric clinic, I usually only saw Mom on the weekends. I was glad for an extra pair of eyes to look out for her.

Actually, I hadn't heard from Becky in a while, not since before Mia moved back home after graduating from the University of California. She wanted to get her own place, but was paying off her loans and trying to build up some savings. Mom, who was in great health at sixty-five, was lonely after dad died, and hadn't really wanted Mia to move out anyway. I also liked the idea of them living together and taking care of one another, at least until Mia found a job in keeping with her degree and made enough money to move out. I called Mom a couple times a week, and saw her nearly every weekend, but it was reassuring to have Mia in the house with her. Mom was completely self-reliant, but after Dad died I realized how much she had needed him emotionally. She could handle anything, but I also knew she was lonely. Although her pretty smile was still there, it didn't light up her eyes the way it used to. Mia's presence seemed to change that.

Becky called that Saturday morning at about ten a.m. to report that there was a patrol car in front of Mom's. Becky just wanted to know if everything was all right. I told her I didn't know, but that I was sure it was nothing.

I called Mom and got no answer. At that point, I was a little worried, but I figured there must have been some vandalism to Mom's fence again. Twice now Mom had reported spray-painted graffiti on her back fence. Mom was only about four blocks from the high school, and her fence was sometimes used as a canvas for some of the more "artistic" youth in the area.

Brett was in the backyard mowing the lawn, and I had been folding some towels when Becky called. When I didn't get through to Mom on the phone, I decided to drive over there and find out what was going on. I knew that Mom would never have answered the phone if an officer was still there (too rude!) so I wasn't too worried. Of course, if there was something wrong, I wanted to get over there to help. But even if it was nothing, I would still get a break from the housework I had started and an unexpected visit with Mom. I was sure that the officer would be finished at Mom's by the time I got there. Mom and I could have a quick cup of coffee and a chat, and I'd still be back home in a couple hours. God knows, the housework would still be there.

"There just aren't enough hours in the day," I muttered as I went to find Brett in the yard. I quickly gave him the scoop on Becky's call. Brett offered to go (he, like me, would have gladly left the yard work if an excuse presented itself), but I told him to stay home with Kara. If something was wrong, I didn't want Kara underfoot.

I tried calling Mom once more and still got no answer. I hopped in the car and tried to ignore the tickling in the pit of my stomach. "Quit being a worrywart," I said aloud, as I tried to make the twenty-minute drive in fifteen.

When I pulled up, I was surprised to see a second patrol car and a gray sedan parked at the curb. The front door was open, even though it was only about fifty-five degrees out. I walked in, and although it sounds like something you'd see in a movie, it was like time slowed down. I felt my heart beating its steady thud-thud as I registered all the details of the room. I noticed the moment when the light April breeze last touched the nape of my neck and I crossed the threshold into the warmth of mom's home. I noticed the welcoming scent of coffee and the after-shave of one of the officers who had entered the room before me. I saw Mom's cat get up from the back of the couch and stretch in the sun that shone through the window, as if he had just noticed that he had company in the room. I even felt the wooden screen door in my left hand – needs sanding, I thought – and then I was in the living room, where I saw that everyone had stopped talking. I hadn't heard voices as I approached, but the complete silence made me realize that there had been murmurs of quiet conversation prior to my arrival. The feeling in my stomach changed from its earlier tickle to a kind of funny pain, as if the toast I'd nibbled on earlier had developed fingernails and was trying to climb its way back out. My heart continued to beat, and I heard my breath whoosh in and out. I felt removed, as if I was a fly on the wall, although I knew the others in the room could see me and must think I was rude for staring. Still, I had stopped walking and simply stood, afraid to get any closer into the circle of men around my mother. Mom sat in a chair with a uniformed officer standing beside her. Another officer was standing a few feet away, looking uncomfortable. A man in a suit, whom I later learned was Detective Sergeant Walter, was sitting in one of our dining-room chairs, which had been positioned directly in front of Mom. He was holding Mom's hand and after a pause he started talking softly to her again, as if he knew I wasn't ready yet to join their conversation.

I shook myself mentally to overcome my sudden laryngitis. I'd never had trouble talking before, for God's sake. "Mom, what's going on?" I asked. My voice came out shakier than I'd expected, but at least it came out. Mom slowly raised her eyes to mine as if my voice had finally reached her through a sea of Jell-O. She spoke so quietly that I could barely hear her. When I just looked at her, bewildered, she repeated her words, louder this time.

"Mia's dead," she whispered. I couldn't deny this time that I had heard her correctly. And just like that, my life changed forever.

I don't remember the next few minutes very clearly. I know I suddenly felt very light-headed and nauseous. I started to walk towards my mom, but the next thing I knew I was sitting on the couch. The officer who smelled nice was handing me water and asking if I felt better. Mom came and sat next to me on the couch. We sat there holding onto one another's hands like they were ropes in quicksand. Sergeant Walter, who looked strong enough to pull us out with that rope, took over.

"I know this is hard, probably the hardest thing you both will ever go through," he said. "I promise you, you are stronger than you know, and you will handle this. We'll help you." He looked straight into our faces with his dark brown eyes, and I wanted to believe him. I decided to convert to The Church of I Can Handle This and It Will Be All Right. I wanted the strength I saw in Sergeant Walter's eyes. Yesterday, I would have bet that I'd had it. Today, everything was different.

**It's** funny how we measure our lives by the "before" and the "after." Like, "before we got married" and "before we had kids." The "befores" and the "afters" change, depending on what's going on in our lives. But the "after" in "after Mia died" has remained the permanent dividing line between my old and new life.

By the end of the day on April twenty-third, this is what I knew:

Mia had gone to work the day before as usual. She worked at the Bun in the Oven, where she did a bit of everything but the cooking, and she usually didn't get home until a little after four. Before she left for work, Mia said that she might get together with her good friend Laura for a night out. It wasn't firmed up, but if they went out Mia said she would probably stay the night at Laura's. This was usual for Mia because Laura had a place in town close by where they liked to go dancing. Mia was very responsible about not drinking and driving, and from there it was easy enough to either walk or share a taxi to Laura's after a night's outing.

So when Mia didn't come home that night, Mom assumed she was with Laura. She didn't worry about Mia and Laura, because they were both responsible girls. They liked to have a few drinks and go dancing a couple times a month, usually right after they got paid. Laura worked in a downtown clothing store and since both girls mostly worked weekends and had to be up early, they were fairly conservative partiers for twenty-four year olds.

"The last thing she said before she left was "I love you," Mom told me. What a small blessing, I thought. At least Mom and Mia got to say "I love you" to one another on Mia's last day.

Mia's car was found on Holcomb road, about five miles from town at about six o'clock Saturday morning. It was parked on the side of the road with the keys in the ignition. The doors were locked and the off-duty officer who saw it while he drove home after his shift figured that the driver must have locked him or herself out. The car checked clear with Dispatch and since the officer had come from town, he figured he'd just keep an eye out for the driver on his way down the road. He didn't encounter anyone, but it was too early to go knocking on doors for no reason. Thinking nothing of it, the officer let the radio dispatcher know the car's location and went home.

About two hours later, a runner in training for a cross-country meet was jogging through the White

Church Woods. The woods start off behind an old church, on the east side of the city limits and go back about eight miles east to the base of Mt. Winston,– almost as wide as they are deep. Most people who want to hike Mt. Winston follow the road just outside the woods and park at its base. Some people walk or bike on some of the trails that start at the front of the woods. But the trails only go two miles back and then veer to the side toward a small lake just north of the woods. Opposite the lake, the trails all end and there's nothing to see but trees, trees, and more trees. While it's common to see people hanging out around the woods, not too many people go very deep into them.

But on this particular morning a runner wanted to increase his stamina by sprinting uphill, so he was willing to run through the woods to get to the base of the mountain. When he was well into his sixth mile, and into the deep woods, he saw a flash of yellow. It was too bright to have been a flower and when he ran over for a closer look, he saw an ankle just above a yellow ballet flat. The police were on the scene less than an hour later.

My sister's identification was not on her body. However, since Middleton is a relatively small city, the dispatcher remembered the abandoned red Honda that was registered to a female, and the police connected the dots. Someone knew that Mia worked at the Bun in the Oven. They took a Polaroid of my sister's face and showed it to the manager of the restaurant in order to make a positive identification. No one wanted to scare Mom if Mia had just had car trouble and gone home with a friend.

After confirming that the dead girl was indeed Mia Hunt, the police went to see Mom. We didn't know much those first few days. We were told that an autopsy would be conducted. After the autopsy was completed, Mia's body could be released and we could plan the funeral. Robert and his wife Cindy came from Illinois. They left their kids with Cindy's mom and stayed in Robert's old room at Mom's.

I was ashamed of myself for falling apart early on, when Mom stayed so strong. I tried to redeem myself by being the strong one while we waited for the autopsy to be completed. I spent a lot of time hovering around Mom and trying to take care of her. In truth, Robert, Mom and I mostly clung together in the kitchen of the house. Friends and neighbors brought wonderful food that we ate when prodded to do so ("to keep up your strength," they said), but nothing had any taste.

Brett was wonderful. He took over all the things I just couldn't handle those first couple weeks, which meant pretty much everything. Luckily, there was no need for cooking that first week at least, because of all the casseroles that had taken up residence at Mom's. I took two weeks off work, and my boss told me to take another week if I needed to.

I was worried about Kara, but she seemed to be doing okay. She was too little to suspect that her parents would ever lie to her. When we told her that Aunt Mia was an angel in heaven now, she pretty much took it in stride. She cried a little bit at first, when we told her that we wouldn't see Mia again until we were very old and went to heaven. She had really wanted Mia to come with us on the first day of kindergarten in the fall. But we told her that Aunt Mia could still see her and would watch over her. Once Kara was assured that she could still show Mia things, and talk to her (even though humans can't hear angels answer), she was placated. We kept her out of school for three days and on her first Friday back she came home pretty excited. She said she was the only one in her class with an Aunt who was an "angel in heaven." The only time she seemed to really get upset was when she saw her grandma cry, so we tried to hide it from her as best we could.

Mia's body was released from the Medical Examiner's on April twenty-fifth. We had the funeral four days later at our family church, First Methodist. Brett and I were members there, but we didn't go as often as we felt we should. None of that seemed to matter when we entered the church for Mia's service. The funeral was standing-room only. It wasn't really surprising because Mia was popular and loved. But there were also a lot of people who attended who had never met Mia. We didn't have a lot of murders in Middleton. Mia had been young, pretty, and from a good family. It frightened people to their bones that this could happen in our town. If it had happened to Mia, it could have happened to any one of their daughters, girlfriends, or friends. So everyone came to show their support, all the while thanking God that

21

this had happened to us, instead of to them.

It had only been a week, but the police had no leads. All we had been told was that Mia had died from "Homicidal Violence." The man who had found her body had been cleared because Mia's time of death was ruled between eleven p.m. and three a.m. The man who found her had actually been out of town on business in Oregon during the three days prior to her death. His wife accompanied him, since her folks lived down in Portland. They had driven home late Friday night, and hadn't arrived back in Middleton until after midnight. The man's wife swore that he was in bed with her all night until he got up early to go running. There seemed no reason to doubt either of them.

When the police checked with Mia's friend Laura, she told them that they hadn't gone out that night after all. Mia had worked later than usual and she didn't close the shop until almost seven. She told Laura that she was tired and wanted to go home and relax. They agreed to touch base on Saturday and possibly go out Saturday night. They chatted a bit before hanging up, and Mia told Laura she was going to run by Target to get some toiletries and maybe go to the video store. Just a quiet night, she told her friend.

The police were able to verify that Mia went to Target. She purchased some toothpaste and tampons and lip gloss, and the new People magazine. She left there at seven-twenty p.m. There was no hint of trouble on the video surveillance. She didn't go to the video store. No one was sure whether she was the one who left her car out on Holcomb road, or if someone else had driven it there later.

Holcomb road led away from both Mom's house, and from the woods where Mia was found. Mom, who was deeply religious, took solace in her faith. She looked terrible, and was visibly sad, but also seemed somewhat at peace. Don't get me wrong, she was devastated that Mia was dead. But she truly believed that Mia was happy in heaven and it gave her comfort that Mia was with Dad. Mom had never been one to dwell on what she couldn't change. Finding Mia's murderer wouldn't bring her back. She focused on the living. She worried about Robert and me and our families. She worried about the man who had found Mia and how he was handling things, and kept him in her prayers. Mom was from a generation that expected life to be hard. She would not second-guess God. I was in awe of her strength and ability to trust that this was part of God's plan. Following her example, I prayed and prayed for a peace that didn't come. I knew that God didn't want Mia to die. I believed with all of my heart that the evil son-of-a-bitch who had killed her needed to be caught and punished. I trusted that when the police caught him and he was convicted and sent to prison, that our family could start to really heal.

I had started to dream about Mia regularly after the funeral. Not every night, but about once a week or so. Luckily, they were the same happy dreams that were basically just memories from our childhood.

One time, I dreamed about Mia's attempt to make enough money for some new shoes that Mom refused to buy. They were too expensive, and Mom insisted that Mia had perfectly good shoes. It was summer and Mia was seven. She wanted those shoes more than she'd ever wanted anything. She asked mom for permission to set up a lemonade stand on the sidewalk in front of our house to earn money for the shoes. Mom warned her that she would never be able to earn enough for the shoes, but Mia begged for the chance to try and Mom finally gave her permission.

Mia ended up selling grape Kool-Aid, because Mom was busy and Mia could make that herself. Mia had been out there about three hours while Mom kept an eye out for her from the kitchen window. Mom made Mia come in for lunch, but then Mia went right back outside. She spent a total of six hours selling her Kool-Aid that day and Mom was proud of her for working so hard. When Mom made her quit and come in for dinner, she was almost ready to make an offer to pay the difference for the shoes, since Mia had worked so hard. But when Mia came in, she had fifty-two dollars. The shoes were forty-five dollars. We were all shocked! How had Mia made that kind of money? Mom went ahead and took Mia to buy the shoes, and we all made jokes about how she was a natural born salesgirl. All was well and everyone was proud. Until Sunday, when several people approached mom in church. They all wanted to tell her how wonderful it was that Mia was doing fund-raising to buy that needy little girl a pair of shoes. Mom was mortified. As soon as she got Mia out of church, Mom asked her what the women were talking about.

"Mia Elizabeth Hunt, tell me this minute what you said to those people to get them to buy your Lemonade!" Mom fumed.

"Mama, it was Kool-Aid," Mia answered, trying to delay the inevitable.

"Don't you get smart with me! What did you tell them?"

Mia smiled her sweetest smile. "Well, Mama, I put a sign up. It said, Raising Money for a Girl Who Can't Afford New Shoes. Please Help." Mia batted her eyes, because she knew she hadn't technically lied, and she figured that she couldn't be punished unless she lied. Mom just looked at Mia as if she was about to say something. After a pause she told Mia to go get in the car with me, and she would be right there. Mom came to the car a few minutes later in what seemed to be a great mood. I saw Mia visibly relax. Mom told Mia she was proud of her for thinking of a way to raise money. Mia beamed. She had gotten her money, her shoes, and had escaped Mom's anger. I was almost eighteen at the time, and knew better. I waited for the punch line. "I told Pastor Sinclair that you had a lot of success with your Lemonade stand," Mom went on. "He suggested that you continue to raise money on the weekends for the rest of the month for the Church Food Bank Fund. Luckily, there are two more Saturdays left in the month. You can have two more all-day lemonade stands and give all the money you make to Pastor Sinclair for the Food Bank. It's so lucky that you showed us how to make money for the poor with your lemonade stand, Mia."

"Kool-Aid stand, Mama," Mia said, sadly. I was sitting in the front seat and my sideways glance caught both Mia's look of defeat, and Mom's look of satisfaction for yet another perfectly meted out punishment. Mom was always the master. In some families, the dad doles out the punishment, but in our family, it was Mom. Dad had kind of taken charge of Robert, but since the youngest two children were girls, and Mom could see that Dad basically couldn't deny us anything, she took over. Oh, you could try to go around Mom to Dad, but it wasn't worth it. As I said, Mom was the master at meting out a punishment that would both teach you a lesson, and make you feel truly guilty about what you had done in the first place. That's why we were both pretty good girls. Mom loved us so much, and was so proud of us, that when we did something really bad – ethically or morally wrong, a lie or a cheat -- it hurt her to her core. And it was never worth it, because we always got caught.

In later years, the family teased Mia about her Kool-Aid Caper mercilessly and she always laughed the loudest. That was a good dream. I actually woke up with a bubble of laughter escaping from my throat.

I had been back to work for a month, and things were good even though people were still so careful around me. I could feel them walking on eggshells a bit, but I knew they really just cared about how I was doing. And it was good to stay busy. I was glad to have my work to distract me slightly from what was now a familiar ache deep in my chest. It was worse when I actively thought about Mia, but even at my busiest, it was always there. It was a like a black hole in space, so heavy and dark that it consumed all the light around it. I could keep it in check by staying busy, and my daughter's hugs and kisses could keep it corralled within the borders it currently occupied. But if I had too much quiet time to think, it started to grow. I thought that eventually I could get that ache to shrink, or that maybe I could capture it in a smaller box, where I would be able to lift the lid and embrace the grief at appropriate moments. No more crying in the grocery store checkout because a girl Mia's age was buying beer and chips with her friends. No more sobbing when I read in the paper that someone in Mia's class had gotten married. Someday, I thought, I will be able to focus on the happy memories. All this crying and sadness and feeling like the world had lost its shine was normal, I knew. It hadn't been very long, just a month or so. Someday I would be able to get it in the box, and keep it there. But for then it was all I could do to keep the black hole from growing.

Work was a blessing. As the office manager at the Middleton Pediatric Clinic, I was on the phone a lot of the time. I also checked in the patients for Dr. Mitchell and Dr. Carnegie. Most of the patients' parents (who were my age) knew I was the sister of the murdered girl. They tended to look at me with pity, which I appreciated the first two weeks I was back. After that however, it started to piss me off. I didn't know why, but I figured that anger was a step in the right direction. I knew I wasn't really angry at them (I had watched THAT much Oprah!) so I tried to kill the looks of pity with overzealous friendliness. I could out-friendly anyone, when I set my mind to it. I'm sure everyone at work thought I was incredibly brave, or maybe slightly crazy. My coping mechanism was to act the opposite of how I felt. The sadder I felt, the happier and more friendly I acted towards the patients and my coworkers. On really bad days, I was perky to the point of obnoxiousness.

Although I was functioning well, there was something new going on with how I was feeling in general. I was not an angry person. I never had been. And I hadn't been acting angry. But something had changed in the last few weeks. I was FEELING very angry, and I was starting to feel a little bit taken aback at just how angry I felt inside. Not all the time, and not only in reaction to well-meaning looks of pity. Just in general. I tried to identify and label this feeling. It was not quite "rage" because I didn't feel compelled to act on it. It was like something was brewing. I settled on the word "seething." That seemed to hit the nail on the head. I was actually seething. Very un-Kate-like seething. I had always been pretty even-tempered. I knew that anger was one of the steps of grief (there was a brochure at the funeral home), although I couldn't have told you which one. I knew I was rightfully angry at the murderer and probably at life in general, and maybe even at God, for letting Mia die. But this was a new level of anger for me, and it was disconcerting. Hmmm, I thought. I had better get a handle on that. All this anger. I made a mental note to look into meditation. Maybe that would help.

But I was pretty confident that whatever I was feeling was normal. I have never been one to doubt myself too much. I was cooking, cleaning, working, and taking care of my family. I was confident that once the police found and convicted Mia's killer, I would slowly start to get back to normal. Life went on. My days were busy and at night the dreams of Mia continued. Sometimes I had them several days a week, and sometimes two weeks would go by before I would dream of her again. The dreams continued their pattern of happy memories until Mia had been dead about seven weeks. It was then that something shifted.

That first night, seven weeks after Mia's death, I dreamed about her high school prom. Mia's boyfriend had broken up with her at the end of March of that year. They had dated almost a year, and she was pretty sad. But Mia was also a very glass-half-full girl. She was busy with college plans and excited about the future. She wasn't dating anyone new, but was busy every weekend with group activities.

On April first, Jonathan Stuber had surprised Mia by asking her to the prom. He walked up to her locker at the end of the day and simply said, "Mia, will you go to Prom with me?" Jonathan was a nice boy, but was almost cripplingly shy. He was known to smile with downcast eyes at those whom he liked. Most people had never heard him speak more than a sentence at a time. He was a straight A student, but was pretty socially inept. He had never gone to a school dance, and he seemed content to hang out with his two best friends from the Math Club. He was a nice looking boy -- one of those kids who wasn't disliked in school, but was pretty much invisible. Half the kids in class had gone to school with him for four years, but couldn't have told you his name.

Mia was, she later admitted, shocked. Even so, she recognized the fear in Jonathan's eyes. "Sure," she said, and they exchanged phone numbers so they could coordinate the date.

Later, some of Mia's friends told her she should find an excuse not to go with Jonathan. There was talk of several boys who had hoped to ask Mia to Prom, but they had been holding off until it was clear that she and her boyfriend were really through. Prom was all about "your" group of friends sharing a limo, and going to the dinner and dance together. This Jonathan guy was an outsider. He wouldn't be comfortable. It wouldn't be fair to him! And Mia might even be expected to go along with Jonathan's group of math geeks.

Mia was only human. She was disappointed about having said yes to a boy she didn't have feelings for, and who didn't know any of her friends. In the dream I caught her crying after getting off the phone with her best friend, who had been begging her to reconsider her choice in prom date.

I asked Mia what she was going to do. Mia responded with a maturity that I had no idea she possessed. "Kate, we had this speaker in class during sophomore year. It was this guy who graduated like fifteen years ago. It was right after that one kid got beat up after school and all the parents freaked out. So we had an assembly on bullying."

"This guy looked just like a normal guy. But he said that high school was hell for him. He said he was a nerd in high school and didn't have any friends. He said a good day was when everyone just ignored him and no one made fun of him. Katie, it shaped his whole life!"

Mia's eyes filled with tears. "He tried to kill himself during his senior year. Do you know why? Because he was about to graduate, and he felt like a total outcast! He felt like the rest of his life was just going to be more of the same." Mia was fired up now. I could feel her shift from sadness to lecture mode. "What is wrong with people? How can they be so mean? That poor man said it took him until he was almost thirty before he started to really feel that he had some self-worth. And this wasn't some kid who was abused at home. All his insecurities came from how he was treated in school! Jonathan is a nice guy. He isn't that popular, but he is polite and has a good heart. Why should I hurt him? What makes me so special that I would think that I am too good to go to Prom with him? You should have seen his eyes, Katie. He was scared to death that I'd say no. But he still asked. So he's brave, too. I'm going with Jonathan and anyone who doesn't like it can just kiss my ass!"

I must have looked shocked because Mia dissolved into laughter, rolling around on the bed with tears still in her eyes. I laughed, too, and made kissing noises in the general direction of her butt. But I was so proud of her. My baby sister was growing up.

In my dream, I saw Mia and Jonathan walk to the limo, just as it really happened, and then I abruptly awoke with a feeling of disquiet. It was a happy dream, and I should have enjoyed remembering how proud I was of my sister. For some reason, though, the dream had disturbed me. I lay in bed mulling it over for a few minutes until I got disgusted and gave myself a good mental shake. Honestly, what did I expect, to feel happy remembering how wonderful Mia was? She was truly special, and would have brightened the world in a thousand ways if not for the monster who stole her away from it. Of course I felt disturbed.

I glanced at the bedside clock and saw it was just after two a.m. I willed myself to get back to sleep. My last thought before drifting off was that I would call Sergeant Walter in the morning and see if there had been any progress in the investigation.

Kara had a doctor's appointment the next morning for a checkup and I had taken the day off of work. From experience, I knew that by the time I got her out of the doctor's and had fed her lunch, it would be too late to take her to preschool. I thought it might be nice for us to have a weekday off, so we played hooky together. After her appointment I took her to Dairy Barn for lunch, where she had the kids' meal with chicken strips, and I had an Ultimate Burger. Kara, in keeping with her love of all things pink, had a small strawberry sundae for dessert and I had an Oreo Cookie blizzard. It felt good to sit in the sun with my daughter, eating ice cream. Afterwards, I took her to the park, where I pushed her on the swing and watched her go down the slide about fifty times. Then we played on the see-saw, which was a good workout for my legs, and I hoped, helped to off-set all that ice cream. We didn't get home until late in the afternoon, and we were both tired. Kara still took an afternoon nap once in awhile, although less and less those days. She had almost fallen asleep in the car on the way home, so I had her lay down for a little while when we got home. For once she didn't argue too much. She was just happy to be at home on a school day. I promised to wake her up in an hour so she could watch her favorite show on TV.

Now was my chance to call Sergeant Walter.

I was in luck and reached him at his desk. I asked if there was any news and he said they were still waiting for the results from the forensic tests. When I asked what they were looking for, Sergeant Walter sounded uncomfortable, but said, "Body fluids." Of course I had considered the fact that Mia may have been raped, but I hadn't ever actually asked about it. Although I thought I was ready now to hear the answer, the idea of it made me sick.

With more assertiveness than was characteristic for me, I asked Sergeant Walter when my family would have access to the autopsy report. After a pause, Sergeant Walter said that we would not get access to that. I told him that I thought we had the right to know the exact way that Mia had died. With a patience that led me to believe that he had been down this road before, Sergeant Walter said that we could not be given access to the case file information during an active investigation. He told me that detectives were working hard on this case. They had interviewed everyone Mia worked with, and most of her friends, but there was nothing new to report. He urged me to try and concentrate on taking care of myself and my family, and to trust the police to complete the investigation.

I hung up feeling restless and dissatisfied. Don't get me wrong. I had the utmost respect for Sergeant Walter. I knew that he and his detectives were working hard on Mia's case. But the killer was out there. I reminded myself that it hadn't been that long, not even two months. I knew they would get him eventually. I resolved to concentrate on my family. I still believed that once the murderer was caught, convicted, and sent to prison, our family could start to really heal. And maybe I was right. Maybe I would have been able to get on with my life if that had happened. But it didn't. And that's what started me on the path that led me here.

**Mia's** killer was caught during the Fourth of July weekend. Sergeant Walter called me on the morning of the fifth. He asked me if Brett and I, and Mom, could come down to his office. He had news about the investigation. Robert and his family were back home in Illinois and I figured I'd call him after I knew what this "news" was. No sense getting his hopes up until I knew what was going on. Brett and I asked our neighbor Lindsay to watch Kara for a couple hours and headed out nervously.

Brett and I hardly spoke during the drive to Mom's. As we pulled into the driveway he held my hand and told me not to get my hopes up. We didn't know what Sergeant Walter was going to tell us. Some of my newfound anger was ready to show itself. "I'm not an idiot, Brett," I snapped. Brett didn't respond. We had called Mom and told her we were on the way, so she met us in the drive. Brett turned up the radio so we could ride the rest of the way without speaking.

We arrived at Sergeant Walter's office on the second floor of the Criminal Justice Center in downtown Middleton after ten in the morning. He took us to a conference room and offered us each a bottle of water. I took mine gratefully, both because my mouth had suddenly gone dry, and because holding the bottle gave me something to do with my hands.

Sergeant Walter looked somber. I didn't think this was going to be good news.

He greeted us all and asked how we had been holding up. There was a minute or two of chit-chat about Kara and Sergeant Walter's son, who was in the third grade. When we appeared sufficiently braced, Sergeant Walter began. "I have news for you. We have a man in custody for your sister's murder." He appeared to be ready to say more, but was interrupted by our excited comments. "That's great! Who is he?" "Are you sure?" Mom began to cry and Brett and I got up to hug her. We all took a deep breath and composed ourselves. Brett appeared downright thrilled. I felt pretty happy myself, considering. Mom just looked worn out.

Sergeant Walter went on. "His name is Gary Mortenson. Does that name mean anything to you?" We all said we had never heard of the man. Sergeant Walter nodded as if he had expected this. Sergeant Walter said that Mortenson had been stopped for expired license plate tabs by an officer the night before. He had a valid license and no warrants. Sergeant Walter breathed deeply and blinked hard. I didn't understand why he wasn't happier.

This was the news we had been praying for!

"There was evidence found in the trunk of Mortenson's car that clearly ties him to the crime." Sergeant Walter continued. "Mortenson was arrested and interviewed. He made a few statements that indicated he was involved in the crime, before asking for an attorney."

I still didn't understand. Sergeant Walter looked miserable. They had the right man. What was wrong?

"The officer who made the stop is a newer officer. He's very hard-working, but doesn't have much experience. Although we've booked Mortenson on Investigation of Murder, I anticipate that the prosecutor may have some legal concerns with regard to filing charges. Or I should say, I anticipate some issues will be brought forth by defense counsel after charges are filed."

"I don't understand," Brett said. "What legal concerns?"

"Well," Sergeant Walter explained, "the officer had his reasons for arresting Mortenson and searching his vehicle, but he may have pushed the envelope a bit in regard to the search.   Mortenson was cooperative with the officer when he was stopped. The officer got a bad feeling about him though, and now of course we know why. But at the time, it was just a feeling that Mortenson was hiding something. Unfortunately, it was just Mortenson's emotional demeanor, not his actions, that caused the officer to feel this way. Because Officer Ryan felt strongly that Mortenson was hiding something, he asked for permission to search Mortenson's vehicle. Mortenson refused to give permission and started to get a little jumpy. Officer Ryan handcuffed Mortenson for safety purposes. Then Mortenson started repeating that he was refusing to allow a search of his vehicle. Officer Ryan suspected narcotics or possibly weapons were hidden in the vehicle."

"OK," I said. "So what's the problem?"

"Well, Kate, search and seizure laws are pretty strict. Officer Ryan searched Mortenson's vehicle, including the trunk. There's a good possibility that a judge might find that Ryan overstepped his bounds in searching the vehicle. But he did find evidence in the trunk that Mortenson was involved in Mia's murder."

Damn it! Why didn't he get to the point? Couldn't he see we were jumping out of our skins? "What evidence? What was in the trunk?" I asked.

"I can't get into too much detail, but Mia's driver's license and an item of women's underwear were found in the trunk. There was also a knife that appears to have been used in an assault which we suspect will have Mia's DNA on it. Then there were other items that we believe will connect Mortenson to the crime, after DNA analysis."

"Blood. You mean blood. On the knife." I knew I was stating the obvious, but for some reason I needed verification that I understood correctly.

"Yes." Sergeant Walter looked at each of us. "I'm sorry. I know this is very difficult."

Mom hadn't said a word. Now she spoke calmly. "What was in the trunk, besides Mia's license and underwear and the knife?" For just a moment, Sergeant

Walter looked very tired. He took a drink of his water and seemed to regroup. "Ma'am, the details of an investigation like this are always very upsetting. The police also have to keep some aspects of the evidence private to maintain the integrity of the investigation. If I were to give you all the details, it would upset you, and it could also jeopardize the case against Mortenson. Please trust me when I tell you that it's better that you don't know all the details, at least at this time."

Then I chimed in. "Sergeant, remember when I asked you for the results of the autopsy and you said we couldn't have them? Can you appreciate that we need to know this information now?"

"Kate, I do fully understand that you want to know this information. But I have years of experience with murder investigations. You have to trust me on this." He seemed to hesitate for a moment, then added, "I asked you down here today because I know this case got a lot of media attention, and I wanted you to hear the information from me right away. I also want you to prepare yourself for the possibility that reporters might try to contact you for a comment. Remember, you are under no obligation to speak to them."

I sensed that our meeting was coming to an end. It had only been fifteen minutes long, but I felt exhausted. Mom looked like we would have to carry her out of there.

But I couldn't stop myself from asking one more question. "What happens now?"

Sergeant Walter seemed to hesitate again before he spoke. "We're almost positive that Mortenson is the man who killed your sister. We have requested some rush DNA testing to determine whether the items located in his trunk belonged to Mia. I anticipate that we will be asking for a charge of Murder One on Mr. Mortenson. But I want to caution you, there are some questions about the search of the vehicle that might cause us problems. I'm not trying to discourage you, but I want you to be prepared either way."

I still didn't really understand what Sergeant Walter was saying. Was he trying to make us understand that it might be hard to prove that Mortenson did it? It sounded pretty clear cut to me if he had Mia's things in his vehicle. Plus, he had obviously made statements implicating himself in the crime when he was arrested. I understood that sometimes evidence was thrown out but I was too tired to think too much about it then. And Mom looked like she had been run over with a truck.

We thanked Sergeant Walter, who promised to keep in touch, and went back to the car. Brett and I took Mom out to an early lunch and then drove her home. We went in for coffee and stayed until we were satisfied that she was okay. In truth, Mom was probably doing better than I was. She said she would probably take a short nap and then work in her garden. After we got home, Brett went across the street to get Kara. He told me that he would take her to the park, so that I would have time alone to call Robert, and then maybe rest a little bit, too.

Brett was always considerate that way. We had a good marriage, although I knew that I had been neglecting him since Mia died. We made love now and then, but not as often as we used to. And though I had talked to Brett about almost everything before, more and more I was keeping my thoughts and feelings to myself. It just seemed too hard to say them out loud. As crazy as it sounds, I somehow thought that Brett should just know how I was feeling. I didn't think I should have to explain things to him.

It wasn't as if he hadn't tried to bring up the subject of Mia to me now and then. But if he mentioned a happy memory, I tended to bite his head off because I thought he was insinuating that I should be happy when thinking of Mia. If he brought up her murder, I was equally surly, because he never brought it up at a "good time." Brett was still being his wonderful self, but nothing had taught either of us how to deal with this. And for the first time, Brett was an outsider. I guess I should have considered that maybe Brett needed comfort too, but damn it, Mia was MY sister. Sometimes I could fully recognize that I was being a bitch, but I was powerless to stop it. So Brett withdrew a bit, and I let him. Luckily, we could always agree on our darling Kara, and we made showering her with love even more of a priority than it had been before. I made a mental note to tell Brett how much I appreciated him when he got home. Then I realized that I was only putting off calling Robert. I dreaded it, but I knew it had to be done.

I called Robert and gave him the update. He was happy and relieved about the arrest, but didn't seem to want to talk too much about it. Robert had always been a typical guy – not too much into talking about emotions. I knew he loved Mia deeply, but I also knew that he would never fully confide in me about how her murder and the investigation had affected him. He was the big brother, and with me at least, that was the role in which he felt the most comfortable. I hoped that he talked to his wife about his feelings, but I wasn't even sure of that. I was also the most comfortable when I thought of him as the big brother, strong and indestructible. It might have been role-playing for each of us, but it was comforting in its own, strange way. He was the only brother I would ever have, and I would always be his little sister. I would now also be his only sister, but it hurt too much to dwell on that thought. So we talked about the arrest and Sergeant Walter and then shifted over to Brett and Kara and school and work and the price of gas.

Our conversation felt like it lasted a long time, but when I looked at the clock after hanging up, I found we had only been on the phone for about twenty-five minutes. Brett and Kara hadn't come back, and I assumed they would be at the park for awhile. I thought about a nap, but I wasn't feeling sleepy. I decided to sit out on the deck and try to relax. I continued with my mantra – once Mortenson was in prison, then we could all get back to normal. Life would be good again.

**Mia's** murder had been big news around Middleton and it didn't take long for the local media to learn of the arrest. Two days after our meeting with Sergeant Walter, I arrived home from the grocery store after work. Kara was over at Mom's for the day. Now that it was summer and preschool had turned into daycare, we occasionally kept Kara home for a day with Grandma. Kara was in heaven running around Mom's garden, looking for caterpillars and picking raspberries. Kara was also Mom's closest grandchild, and Mom loved having her. It especially helped that when they were together I was able to do the grocery shopping without a little helper urging me to buy all those sugary treats that all of us loved and none of us needed. Ice cream, of course, would always be in the house. But I tried to be a reasonably good mom with regard to nutrition. Oatmeal instead of Sugar Mountain Cereal, most of the time. After I got the bags unpacked that day, I planned to drive over and pick up Kara from Mom's.

I had just popped the trunk and stepped out to unload the first bag, when I saw a nice looking man in a suit walking towards me. The story of the arrest had broken the night before on the news, and I had gotten several phone calls immediately afterwards. I rebuffed all the inquiries and had assumed that was the end of it. So I was surprised to see the man I recognized as the Channel Five news guy headed my way. I always thought he seemed nice on television, so I decided to tell him I had no comment with a smile on my face, rather than running for the door. Besides, I had to unload the groceries, and there was no way for a graceful exit.

"Excuse me Ma'am," he said, simultaneously making me feel old, while impressing me with his manners. "I'm Roger Cantrell from Channel Five news. Might I have a word with you?"

Since he had asked so politely, I couldn't help but smile. "Mr. Cantrell, my family has no comment on the police investigation."

"I can appreciate that Ma'am but our viewers also feel the loss of your sister. We got hundreds of emails after her murder, and they are just very interested in how you and your family are doing. Can I give them an update?"

For some reason, although I recognized this as a play on my emotions, I was touched by it. I knew that in the past few months many people had told me they were praying for us. I didn't want to seem ungrateful for the community support. So I told Cantrell that we were doing as well as could be expected, and were happy about the arrest. I guess I shouldn't have let my guard down, because what came next hit me like a kick to my stomach.

"It must have been horrible to learn that her body had been violated that way," Cantrell said, leaning towards me casually. "What was your reaction when you learned that Mortenson kept her body parts in his trunk?"

I know that Cantrell said something after that, but all I heard was an increasing buzzing sound. I must have just stared at him. I noticed that my bag of groceries, previously in my hand, was now askew on the ground. Cantrell was apologizing. Apparently he had SOME sense of conscience. I walked to my front door and unlocked it. The last thing I heard before I shut the door was Cantrell, yelling out an offer to help carry in my groceries. Normally I'm a very polite person. I can be assertive, but I like to think that I'm pretty calm and respectful, even at my most confrontational. Well, not that day.

I went into the living room and called Sergeant Walter's line. Obviously, the man wasn't a psychic, or he would never have answered. His mistake.

"Homicide, Sergeant Walter," he said when he answered.

"Sergeant. This is Kate. What the FUCK do you think you were doing, leaving out that little tidbit of information about Mia's BODY PARTS in the trunk, during our meeting? Why the HELL did you call us down there for our little meeting, so that we could hear the news from you first, if you were going to let the media know all the gory details to throw in our faces a day later?

As you can imagine, I was just fucking thrilled to pull into my driveway and get asked about my sister's fucking BODY PARTS!" A bit calmer now, but still vibrating with anger, I choked out, "You WILL tell me what was in that trunk and you WILL tell me now!" Unfortunately, my tough guy routine was undone by the fact that I had started sobbing uncontrollably into the phone.

Sergeant Walter, God bless him, didn't seem to be startled or offended by my rant. "Kate, I'm so sorry you found out this way. The media wasn't supposed to get that information either. I'm very unhappy about this." He paused, and I felt that he really WAS pretty angry about the leak. It reminded me that he and I were, after all, on the same side. Sergeant Walter went on in a soft voice. "I would like to come out and meet with you and your husband and explain, if that's okay. I don't know if your mom will want to be there. This is a pretty upsetting subject. How about if I stop by and talk with you and Brett tonight, and you can decide afterwards whether you want me to meet with your mom, too?"

After I agreed and we set a time to meet I calmed myself down and called my mom to ask if she could keep Kara for dinner. I called Brett on his cell and told him that Sergeant Walter would be by at six-thirty and I looked outside to make sure that Cantrell was gone. When I saw the yard was clear I went and got my groceries from the trunk. The eggs were in the sack I dropped (Murphy's Law) and were broken. I got all the bags into the kitchen and unpacked them. Then I sat down to wait for Brett and Sergeant Walter to arrive, and for my world to fall apart, again.

Sergeant Walter arrived a little after six that evening. I could see him parked just north of our house. I could have been friendly and waved him in, but I decided he could sit in his car for a few minutes. Childish and petty? You bet. But I was still feeling pretty angry. I had been ambushed in my driveway. And now I had to make a second trip to the store just to replace the broken eggs. I needed to blame someone, and he was within range! And it had worked. Sergeant Walter was going to give me the answers I wanted. I quieted the "be careful what you wish for" warning that ran through my mind, and concentrated instead on reminding myself to control my temper tonight. I didn't want to alienate the Sergeant. He was our link to the police investigation. Besides, I thought, he really was a nice guy. I could tell he legitimately cared about our family and how we were doing.

At six-thirty on the nose, Sergeant Walter exited his Crown Victoria and walked to the door. He knocked and I answered as Brett came out of the kitchen. "Hello, Sergeant," Brett said. "Thank you for coming. Kate had quite a shock earlier. Apparently that news guy knows a lot more than we do. We're hoping you can clear that up."

I was pleased that Brett appeared sane and rational. He had been upset when I told him what Cantrell had said, but he was mostly upset about Cantrell's conduct and the way I had been confronted. Brett must have learned something by watching all those Law and

Order re-runs, because he wasn't shocked at the content of Cantrell's disclosure. Brett was a bit of a true-crime buff, but nothing excessive. Apparently, though, Brett was not surprised to hear Mia's killer had her body parts and he was able to discuss it calmly with Sergeant Walter, without even one use of the "F" word. Brett and I really need some quality time alone, I thought. There are some things I never would have guessed about my husband. His knowledge that killers kept body parts was one of those things.

I recovered my manners in time to offer Sergeant Walter coffee, which he accepted. I really did feel a little sorry for the man. I knew it was after work hours, and realized the long hours he was putting into this investigation. Now, it seemed, he was also missing dinner with his family to talk about body parts with mine.

When we all had our coffee, Sergeant Walter took the initiative. "Kate, let me say again how sorry I am that you heard the news that way. We try to maintain secrecy around the details of the evidence. There are good reasons for that. The killer should be the only one who knows the exact details of the crime. That way, when he talks about them and gives the correct details, it helps us prove he committed the crime. But when the media gives out the specifics, a defense attorney could argue that we obtained a false confession, because all the details had been broadcasted earlier. That's one of the reasons I didn't go into detail with you and your mom about what was in the trunk."

He took a sip of coffee, then added, "The other reason is that I didn't want to needlessly upset you and your family. I don't know who gave Cantrell his information. No one in the department authorized its disclosure. If I knew that information had been leaked, I would have warned you ahead of time. Again, I'm very sorry about the way this played out."

I was surprised to feel that my anger was gone and had been replaced by a giant lump in my throat. I was on the verge of tears again. Geez. Grow up, Kate. I took a sip of my coffee. It squeezed past the lump and burned going down my throat.

"Sergeant, can you please just tell us about the body parts? I don't think I could take any more surprises from the press."

"Okay, I know this is very upsetting," Sergeant Walter said. I'll try to answer your questions as best I can. When we found Mia's body, some of her flesh had been removed. The areas of missing flesh matched what was found in Mortenson's trunk."

"Sergeant? C'mon. Fingers, feet, her head? What did he take?" Exasperated by the lack of detail, my voice cracked at the last question, and I knew I was about to cry. But I was usually a "rip off the band-aid" kind of girl. I preferred quick, intense pain to prolonged pain.

"We're ready," Brett said. "Just out with it, please." Huh, I thought, Brett really does know me.

Sergeant Walter hesitated a moment, and then said, "I want you to consider something. The only reason I'm willing to share this information with you is because of that leak to the press. I don't want you blind-sided again. But the details are extremely disturbing, and there's a good chance that even the media would find the details too disturbing for their public. I'd like you to consider holding off on asking for this information. If we go to trial, it will all come out at that time."

Sergeant Walter looked at each of us expectantly. Brett gave me a look that I understood meant he would abide by my decision. I knew I might regret this, but my curiosity would not be quieted. I spoke up. "Sergeant, I understand what you're saying. But my imagination is already running wild. We might want to shield my mother from this information. But I can't describe how horrible, I mean truly horrible, it was to be surprised in my driveway like that." I paused, feeling like I needed to gather my strength. I was so very, very tired. "I think it's likely we'll find out the details at some point anyway. I'd prefer to have some control, however slight, over the circumstances in learning about this. Please just tell us." I gave a half-smile, trying my best to appear calm and ready for anything. My stomach was flip-flopping like a pancake chef during the breakfast rush, and I noticed my hand shook slightly as I picked up my coffee cup. I was sure that I hadn't fooled the good Sergeant, but he seemed willing to go along with my charade.

"Okay," he said with a look of resignation. "I know you're aware that there was some mutilation. I want you to understand and remember that the Medical Examiner determined that the mutilation occurred after death. Mia didn't feel the things that were done to her body at that point." Sergeant Walter took a drink of coffee and carefully set the cup back down into the saucer. He looked at me, giving me one last chance to change my mind. "Go on," I said bravely (I hoped).

"Mia's breasts had been removed from her body when we found her. We found what we believe is one of her breasts in the trunk of Mortenson's car. Part of her genitals had also been excised from her body. Her pubic hair had been, for lack of a better term, 'scalped' and was also found in Mortenson's trunk. We're still waiting on the DNA results, but there is little question that the recovered flesh is Mia's." He paused and said, "I'm sorry."

I suddenly felt very nauseous. I put my coffee on the table, said, "Excuse," but didn't get out the "me" before I ran to the bathroom and vomited up the remnants from lunch. I rinsed out my mouth with minty mouthwash and tried to avoid the reflection of the pale woman in the mirror. I went back to the living room, where Brett and Sergeant Walter sat in the same positions. They both stood up when I returned, like the gentlemen they were.

"Sorry," I said.

"Not necessary," said Sergeant Walter.

We all sat down and looked at our coffee cups for a moment. "What happened to Mia's other breast?" I finally asked. Brett looked at me, shocked. Apparently he had not done the math. Both of her breasts were cut off, and only one breast was recovered.

Sergeant Walter nodded, as if he had expected this question. "It was recovered with Mia's body."

I was on a roll now, ready to ask the tough questions. No more broken eggs in my driveway. No more surprises. I could take the truth and I would have the truth.

"What did he do with it, after he cut it off?"

Sergeant Walter looked as tired as I had ever seen him. "Kate..." I interrupted. "Please, Sergeant. Out with it."

He obliged. "He covered her face with it."

After Sergeant Walter left, I went straight to bed. Brett was wandering around, looking unsettled. I reminded him to go get Kara and to tell her I loved her. I asked him to tell her that Mommy had a tummy-ache and had to go to bed early. I didn't think I'd sleep, but I was out as soon as my head hit the pillow. I knew then that God was merciful, because I didn't dream at all.

**Mia's** murder and Mortenson's arrest were the top stories on the news for the next few weeks. I learned from Sergeant Walter that Mortenson had a prior arrest for burglary five years ago, but he was never charged. He was also arrested six years ago for voyeurism in California. He was never charged for that offense because the police couldn't prove he was looking into the twenty-one-year-old college student's window for sexual reasons. Mortenson was not a registered sex offender and had never been convicted of a violent crime, and so his DNA was not in the national computer. The police would likely never have considered him a possible suspect in Mia's murder if not for that traffic stop and the possibly illegal search.

As far as the police could tell, Mortenson did not know Mia. No one remembered him eating at the Bun in the Oven. He lived on the other side of town and there was no reason he would have come into routine contact with her. Why he became focused on her was still a mystery. The police speculated that he had just seen her and followed her, maybe even feigning car trouble to get her attention. Mia would have stopped. Everyone who knew her was sure of that fact.

Sergeant Walter also finally told us about the incriminating statements Mortenson made regarding Mia's murder, although he swore us to secrecy. He said that Mortenson admitted owning the car he was driving when he was arrested, and that he was the only one who drove it or had access to the keys for the trunk. We also learned that Mortenson's semen was on my sister's body. For once, I didn't even ask where it was. I assumed it was inside her vagina, but the way he had mutilated her had taught me there are things that go on in this world that I couldn't have even imagined. I decided I really didn't need to know the "where" or the "how." Knowing he had raped her was enough to break my already aching heart ten times over.

We were all happy when Mortenson was charged with First Degree Murder on July seventh. I had a hard time deciding whether to go to the arraignment, mostly because I knew the press would be there, and I didn't want to be the subject of scrutiny. In the end, I felt that I owed it to Mia, and so Brett and I attended the hearing. Mom elected to stay home, but said she would like Brett and me to stop by afterwards and tell her about it so that she didn't have to watch it on the news.

The arraignment was at one o'clock on the ninth floor of the County courthouse. Brett and I got there about thirty minutes early, and walked around in the park outside until twelve-forty-five p.m. When we entered the courtroom, it was almost full. Sergeant Walter had already told us that he wasn't able to attend, and I didn't expect to see anyone I knew. I was surprised to see quite a few members of our church, as well as some of Mia's former co-workers in attendance. The media was there of course, but we did our best to ignore them.

At the very back corner of the room was slight woman who appeared to be in her late seventies, dressed in a gray sweater and matching skirt. Her hair was styled in such a way that I suspected she had fixed it up for this occasion. I had never seen her before, and I suspected she was a relative of Mortenson's. I knew he would have family, of course, but I wasn't sure whether to expect them to support him in court. The woman looked like a typical elderly lady. Maybe she was his mother. If so, there was nothing to indicate that she had raised a killer.

I started to feel a little nauseous as the minutes ticked by. I heard the clerk say that they were ready for the prisoner to be brought over from the jail and I knew I was going to see my sister's murderer for the first time. When I saw him during the earlier news coverage he had been looking down as if to avoid the cameras and all I had seen was a glimpse of a tall man with brown hair. I knew he was evil, and expected that he would look it in person. In my mind's eye I pictured some sort of Charles Manson-like grimace and demeanor, and that his deviancy would be obvious.

I was shocked, then, when Mortenson was escorted into the room by deputies. He was wearing an orange jumpsuit that loudly proclaimed his status as an inmate. The jumpsuit, however, was the only outward clue that he was a criminal. He looked to be in his early thirties and walked with a bit of a limp. He had his head up and quickly looked over the spectators in the gallery, scanning the faces until he found the woman he was seeking in the back row. I was looking at Mortenson, not her, but knew when he found her because he smiled and nodded in her direction. It made me sick to notice that he had a nice smile. He was evil to me because I knew what he had done, but truth be told, he looked just like half the guys in Middleton.

Mortenson's court-appointed attorney made a request for a lowered bail, and mentioned Mortenson's mother Candace, who had been in ill health and was present at the back of the courtroom. Apparently Mortenson routinely drove his mother to and from her chemotherapy sessions and his incarceration had left her without transportation. The judge denied the request, citing the risk to public safety, and after entering a not guilty plea through his attorney, Mortenson was led back to jail.

After the hearing my best friend Lisa, who had been in Europe at the time of Mortenson's arrest, began harping on me to start counseling. Lisa and I went way back, and I loved her but we were as different as night and day. We were the same age, and had met in the third grade over kick-ball. But our lifestyles could not be compared. Lisa was rich (no other way to say it), because she had married a fifty-three-year-old widower when she was twenty-four years old. She seemed to love him at the time, but I had worried about the age difference. They were only married for seven years though, when Lisa's husband had a massive heart attack and died. The estate was split between Lisa and her twenty-one-year-old step-daughter. Contrary to what anyone would expect, Lisa and her step-daughter had always gotten along beautifully, and they continued to have a friendship for years after Lisa's husband's death.

With a large share of the estate Lisa moved to warmer climes in California, and only got back to Middleton occasionally. But we talked on the phone and emailed several times a week. Although she was a "rich widow" as she jokingly called herself, she often told me how she envied me my life. Lisa had wanted a child badly, and had started trying to conceive about six months before her husband's death, without success. Her biological clock was ticking loudly now and at thirty-four she was thinking of adoption if she didn't meet Mr. Right soon. She had the special challenge of meeting men who liked her, not just her money, which is a cliché, but apparently a real problem when you are a single rich girl. Lisa always wanted to hear every detail about Kara, and we had to impart monetary limits on the birthday and Christmas gifts that Lisa was allowed to give. But I was glad that "Aunt Lisa" loved Kara so much, and vice versa.

Lisa had also gone into therapy after her husband's death. She had actually loved him a lot and had a very hard time dealing with his death for awhile afterwards. I tried to help, but I had never known anyone our age who had lost a spouse, and I guess I didn't know the right things to say. The speculation from some in the community that she only married him for his money didn't help. At any rate, therapy was the only thing that did help, and Lisa was a born-again believer in it.

After enduring weeks of Lisa's urgings, I finally started seeing Elizabeth Fuller, who was a counselor at the local hospital, for one hour, once a week. It was actually nice to talk about how I was feeling without having to worry about stressing anyone out. I realized I was spending a lot of energy trying to appear cheerful around Brett and Kara, and even Mom. Elizabeth said it was only natural that the stress would come out in some way. She told me I needed to express my feelings with her. I did, although I was a bit reticent. I'm not really a private person, but she was a complete stranger. So I sugar-coated some of what I said and left out the details of some things that were probably pretty important. Like how I thought of Mia's severed breast one day when I was making spaghetti sauce and got out the big knife to cut the garlic bread. And how I asked Brett if he could cut the garlic bread for me, because the sauce suddenly looked like her blood. Instead of eating that night I took two Advil and went down to throw a load of clothes in the wash because everything suddenly seemed dirty and beyond repair.

60

Yeah, weird stuff. I left most of it out, and just talked about missing my sister. But even that helped, probably because I usually got in a good cry at some point during the session. I had been sleeping fitfully, and it still took me awhile to get to sleep, but it slowly started to get better.

This went on until the beginning of September. Kara started Kindergarten and we were busy at home. The media interest in Mia's death had died down. There were a bunch of behind-the-scenes court appearances that the police victim advocate let us know about, but that seemed to be mostly about scheduling. Things were harder than they were before Mia's death, but they were easier than they had been in July. I felt that if I could just get through the murder trial, everything would be okay.

On September twenty-ninth, Sergeant Walter called. I hadn't heard from him in quite awhile, and I was happy to hear his voice. I knew Brett and Kara and Mom were all safe (we had just gotten back from an early Friday night dinner together) so I couldn't imagine the Sergeant had anything but good news. Maybe just a guilty plea from Mortenson, I hoped silently. But Sergeant Walter asked if he could come and see us. Uh-oh. My heart did a little flip-flop because he didn't sound happy. He said it was important and that he would like to come over now, if that was all right. It was early in the evening, so I told him to come ahead. I called Lindsay next door to ask if she wouldn't mind watching Kara for a couple hours. People had been so nice to all of us ever since Mia died. I hated to take advantage, but sometimes I jumped at the chance and did impose when it was necessary.

Sergeant Walter arrived an hour later and accepted my offer of coffee. We had all just had dinner, but I knew Sergeant Walter was probably late for his, so I put out a plate of cookies. We chit-chatted for a couple minutes, but we were all visibly aware that there was a matter to be discussed. I had enjoyed a good day up until then, and I cowardly decided not to ask any questions or broach the subject of Sergeant Walter's visit. I was going to postpone what I felt sure now was bad news for as long as possible. I knew it wouldn't be long.

After a few minutes Sergeant Walter put down his coffee cup. He explained that the murder charge against Gary Mortenson had been dismissed at a hearing late that afternoon. Sergeant Walter was worried about the press getting the information, and that's why he had wanted to meet with us right away.

I was completely dumbfounded. "What?" I asked.

"Kate, remember when I told you that I thought the legality of the search might cause us problems? Well, it did. The judge dismissed the charge based on the fact that the evidence connecting Mortenson to the crime was found illegally."

"But what about his statements?" Brett asked.

"Everything that came after the illegal search is suppressed because one thing led to another. They call that the 'fruit of the poisonous tree.' The evidence is considered the poisoned fruit of an illegal search. Legally, it's as if he was stopped and ticketed and went on his way. Had the officer not opened the trunk, there would never have been a suspicion that Mortenson was connected to the crime."

He hesitated and then went on. "I'm so sorry. We anticipated this might happen. We've spent the time between his arrest and now, looking for other ways to tie him to the crime. But there is just no separate evidence tying him to your sister. There is something called 'Inevitable Discovery' that means that we could still have charged him, if we had discovered his involvement in another way. For example, if we were interviewing every man your sister dated, and he was one of them, we would have run across him. However, as I said before, there is just no indication that he knew your sister. And since Mortenson's criminal history didn't include anything of this nature, to be honest, he wasn't even on our radar. His DNA was not on file. At this point the only way to charge him is going to be if new evidence arises, or if we get a computer match on his DNA in the future."

"I thought you just said his DNA wasn't on file," I said.

"I'm sorry," Sergeant Walter said. "That was confusing. If Mortenson is convicted of a felony in the future and his DNA entered in the computer, we would get a computer match, tying him to your sister's case. The DNA from the semen found on her body is entered into the computer now, so all we need is that official match. Although we know it's Mortenson's DNA, legally we can't use that information yet. But if his DNA profile is entered into the computer then we can re-charge him."

I was stunned, and I could see that Brett and Mom

were too. "What happens to him now?" Mom asked.

Sergeant Walter sighed. "Unfortunately, he will be released from custody. We will continue to keep an eye on him as best we can. I wish I could assure you that we'll keep twenty-four hour surveillance on him. I actually think that we will, for a time. But it would be unrealistic to think that we will have the manpower and the budget to keep watching him forever. I'm so sorry."

Sergeant Walter leaned forward in his chair. "There's one more thing. Remember the new officer who made the arrest? He's beside himself with guilt. I assure you, he is a fine officer who believed he was justified in making that search. The court decided that he was wrong today. But I pointed out to him, and I want to point out to you, that if he hadn't found Mortenson, we would still not know who murdered your sister. The only good thing that came out of this is that we know who killed her. I am confident that Mortenson will be prosecuted at some point. There is no statute of limitations on murder."

I surprised myself, but I felt absolutely no anger toward the arresting officer. Sergeant Walter was right. If not for him, we would still not know who had killed Mia. And knowing was better than not knowing, no matter what.

"Sergeant, please tell that officer that we don't blame him." I generously added, "Everyone makes mistakes."

"I will. Again, I'm sorry for being the bearer of such bad news. I anticipate that the media will be very interested in this development. You can talk to them if you wish, but you don't have to and they don't have the right to trespass on your property. If you have any problems with that, give us a call. Unless you have any more questions for me, I'll be going now." Sergeant Walter looked at us, but no one spoke. Brett got up and extended his hand to the sergeant. "Thank you for coming and telling us in person. Please keep us informed of any new developments."

"I will, Brett. Thank you for having me in your home. Take care."

I watched Sergeant Walter walk to his car. Suddenly I ran outside. "Wait! I forgot to ask you." I was breathless, which was weird, because I had only run about thirty feet. "Sergeant, when will Mortenson be released?"

Sergeant Walter looked at his watch. "Unfortunately, probably about now. I don't anticipate that he'll seek out any contact with your family. He wants to stay as far away from police attention as he can. I wouldn't be surprised if he leaves town. But if he does approach you, call 911." Sergeant Walter started to get into his car.

"Wait," I said. "Thank you." And then I hugged him, hard. It felt like goodbye, because we both knew that Mortenson had just gotten away with murder. Sergeant Walter got into his car and headed back to what I assumed was a nightmare job. I knew the police department would take a beating in the media for this and I felt my anger building. But strangely, not toward Sergeant Walter or the young officer who had made the arrest. And not for the judge who dismissed the case. All my seething anger was for Gary Mortenson. And I knew I would have to do something about that.

**The** next two weeks were a nightmare. Mia's murder, and Mortenson's arrest and subsequent release were on the news daily. I took the first week off work, because the media tended to wait in the clinic's parking lot both before and after my shift, hoping for an exciting sound-bite from me, or perhaps to see me flip out in time for the five o'clock news. When I went back to work in mid-October, things had quieted down somewhat. I heard there was a lot of buzz about Mortenson's release on the talk-radio station, so I didn't listen to the station at all.

I was having trouble sleeping. I had lost three more pounds, but there was no joy in knowing my body looked slender, because at the top of that body, gazing back at me in the mirror, was my face with a look so sad, so completely heartbroken, that it hurt me to see it. It's hard to explain, but I literally almost didn't recognize myself. If I was an artist or a photographer, and wanted to capture a look of complete devastation, exhaustion, and an absence of hope, I would have sought out my own face. At times, that made me angry, because, selfishly, I didn't want my life to be ruined over this. I wanted things back the way they were. I wanted to be happy. I wanted to laugh. But the rest of the time, I felt so exhausted that I couldn't even work up the energy to be mad.

I knew I was probably on the way to actual clinical depression, and I imagined my future as one of those women who considers it a victory if she can get out of bed in the morning, shower, and go about her day. Still, even recognizing that, I couldn't work up the energy to do anything about it. I got Kara off to school every day, and Brett and I kept the household running (barely) by working together. There were no hobbies, no friendships, no sex life, and no happiness or joy in my life, but for then, that was the way it had to be. The only time I felt the sadness ebb was when Kara would laugh, or crawl up on my lap to tell me some funny story. But Kara had school, and her friends, and her favorite TV show, and as funny as it sounds, she was starting to get her own life. I didn't really try to analyze what was going on with me, but I remember thinking one day that I couldn't cling to Kara forever.

More often than not, when I crawled into bed at night, I thought, "Tomorrow..." I usually didn't finish the thought, but only felt a desperate wish that tomorrow would be better and that I might find some way to be happy.

Brett was sympathetic, but I could tell even he was

losing patience. Still, he kept doing nice things for me in the hopes of making me smile. I started faking smiles for him, but I knew that he recognized them as fake. And he was finally starting to lose his smile too. We made love about once every two weeks, and it wasn't like before. But at least we were doing it, I thought. I knew my marriage was suffering, but at that point, it was just one more thing I felt helpless to fix.

Two days before Thanksgiving, things changed a bit. Kara, my angel, put things into perspective for me. On Tuesday after a fast food dinner because once again I was too tired to cook, Kara came over and kissed my forehead. I was lying on the couch, exhausted after what would have been, in my old life, a pretty easy day at work. Kara had recently announced that she was going to be a doctor when she grew up, and she wanted to take care of me. After the forehead kiss, she announced that I didn't seem to have a fever, and went to get an afghan to cover me. She looked at me with a sympathetic gaze. "Mama, it's okay if we don't have Thanksgiving this year. I know you're too tired. I'm sure you'll feel better by Christmas." Then, in a moment that broke my heart, she added, with worry in her voice, "We can have Christmas, though, right?"

That did it. I hugged her close and told her that of course we would have both Thanksgiving and Christmas. I realized then I had to fix myself. Mortenson had killed Mia and none of us would ever be the same. But I couldn't let this take Kara's childhood. I couldn't let this ruin my family. I had to take my life back. I just wished I knew how.

I called my therapist's office the Monday after Thanksgiving and doubled our appointments to twice a week. Elizabeth offered medication, but I was scared to take it. So we worked on meditation and imagery techniques. For a time it seemed to be helping. I was sleeping better and my energy level was up. But I still felt very sad and afraid. Afraid that someone would kill Kara. Afraid that none of us would ever be safe. I had a constant ache in my shoulders from muscle tension. I realized I was usually physically tensed, ready to fight or run when an attack came. But at least I was sleeping an uninterrupted five hours a night. It beat the two-hours-at-a-time I had been getting for the last several months.

With Elizabeth's encouragement, I did thirty minutes of meditation/deep-breathing with calming imagery every morning and night. I pictured a calm lake with the sounds of birds and the smell of flowers. Honestly, the imagery didn't make me feel calmer, but the idea that I was doing something to try and feel better did. I felt less helpless and more in-charge of my life. But I was still afraid of imminent danger, and still very angry.

Christmas was actually nice. Kara wanted a bicycle and Santa brought it. Mom was emotional on Christmas day, missing both Dad and Mia, but actually seemed to be doing much better than I was. Mom had always been an emotional, heart-on-her-sleeve woman. She could cry and then be fine. I tended to hold things in until I broke, and then took a fair amount of recovery time from my emotional outburst. So I got a bit teary, but luckily didn't go into a complete meltdown that day. It was good to watch Kara so happy, playing with her Barbies and her doctor set. It was good to smell the fragrance of the tree and listen to Christmas music. It felt cozy and safe. Brett had eaten his cinnamon rolls and was dozing in the recliner, waiting for the football game to start. Kara was planning a date between Barbie and Ken. Barbie, who was apparently employed as a doctor, was having a hard time getting time off work to go dancing.

I had just gotten off the phone with Robert, whose own kids were happily playing in the background. We had a couple tears as we said we wished we could all be together during the holidays. After we hung up, Mom and I sat in the kitchen, drinking coffee and reminiscing about Christmases past. We laughed when we talked about how Dad always acted stern and said how "kids today" were spoiled rotten, but then would buy us pretty much everything he could afford to get us from our Christmas wish list. It had been like that for years. Mom would do the Christmas shopping and would get us our number one requested "big" gift, which came from Santa. Mom would then buy us the number two gift, from her and dad. But in the last three days before Christmas, Dad would run out and buy two or three more things for each of us. He never consulted Mom ahead of time, and didn't seem to actually plan to do it. He would just get caught up in the spirit of the season, and run out after work and buy a bunch more gifts. Mom would get disgusted because money was often on the tight side, but Dad just couldn't resist. Then after everything was opened, every year, dad proclaimed that we had gone overboard, and that next year we were going to cut back at Christmastime, and possibly forgo gifts in lieu of volunteering at a shelter. The pattern continued however, until we were grown. Even then, he would call each of us aside at some point on Christmas day, and slip a twenty dollar bill in our hands, telling us to get a little something extra we wanted.

Sitting in my little kitchen, Mom and I actually laughed ourselves to tears at some of the memories. "Katie, remember that year when you were really into Barbie fashion? Third grade or so, right?"

"Something like that, why?" Then suddenly I remembered. It was the year that Barbie turned slutty. Mom and I both started laughing. "Yes!" Mom guffawed. "Starbie!"

Dad, in one of his famous last-minute shopping excursions, had gone to get me some Barbie dresses. But since it was Christmas Eve, all the "good" dresses were sold out. Not knowing a thing about Barbie fashion, other than he needed to go down the Barbie aisle at the store, dad bought three packages of clothing from a cheap imitation, knock-off brand, "Starbie." The dresses looked like they had been peeled off either Las Vegas show-girls, or Las Vegas prostitutes. Dad thought they were marvelous. He positively beamed when I opened my gift. Mom took one look at the leopard skin halter top, matching short-shorts, and stiletto heels, and gasped. Then, she noticed that the accessories included not just the stilettos, but a bottle of wine and a see-through negligee, complete with a feather boa. She grabbed the clothes and told me that no "nice Barbie" would wear such a thing. Dad was heartbroken. He thought the clothing was beautiful. After a discussion between my parents in the other room, I was allowed to have the outfit back, minus the bottle of wine and the negligee. The other two boxes held equally risqué outfits, several items of which my mother withheld from me.

Since I was the oldest girl, and both my parents were pretty protective, my mom actually had a little talk with me the day after Christmas. "Katie, although Ken might like to see Barbie dressed up like that, those clothes are inappropriate. Ken might say he likes her to look like that, but he wouldn't have any respect for her if she wore those clothes. And he might take her on a date, but he would never marry her. Do you understand?" I nodded, although I didn't. I only knew that I shouldn't dress Barbie in the "Jezebel" fashion line (as I heard Mom call it) when Mom was around. But I also loved those stilettos and that red feather boa. After a month or so, mom gained some perspective and laughed about the whole episode. And the whole family laughed one day several months later, when we drove past a very mini-skirted, cleavage-showing female, and I said, "Look, it's Starbie!"

All in all, that first Christmas without Mia was as good as we could have hoped for. That night, I thanked God for giving us a good day. It had been the first one in a long while.

I continued to see Elizabeth once a week into the new year. I was a little frustrated, because I felt stalled in my old patterns. I was still only sleeping about five hours a night, and I was still feeling scared and angry. There were days when I woke up feeling like I wanted to smash every plate in the house, and scream until I lost my voice. There were other days when I woke with my heart pounding, but didn't know why. I felt like I was up against a wall. I needed to find a door to pass through and get on with my life.

By April I was losing patience. I thought I would be a lot better by now. I was still having a lot of fear and anxiety, although I was functioning pretty well. I knew my fears were exaggerated and unreasonable and so I didn't let them change the way I conducted my daily life. But I always FELT wrong, and it was draining to be so stressed and worried. At least my energy level was up from what it had been. But if the phone rang at night, I assumed a loved one had been killed. If I heard a noise, I thought it was a gun shot. I missed the old Kate, who was, if not brave, at least not a coward.

We were coming up on the one year anniversary of Mia's murder. The local papers and TV and radio stations were talking about it again. On one report I saw that Gary Mortenson was working in construction close by. Amazingly, he had his supporters who felt that he was either innocent and had been set up in some way, or that he was guilty but not convicted and therefore excused to live his life. Most people, thankfully, realized that he was a sick, demented rapist and murderer and were disgusted that he was free. I didn't like to hear about Mortenson, but I had paid attention to the reports because I was still afraid of him. After awhile I knew he was living in Belmont, and I knew the name of the company where he worked. I noticed I felt safer when I knew where he was.

It was all still overwhelming and Brett and I decided it was time to take a break. We invited Mom, but she said she was fine and she wanted to stay home so Brett and Kara and I went up to Victoria, British Columbia by ourselves. We soaked up the atmosphere and did all the touristy things. We did not watch the news. We did not talk about Mia or Gary Mortenson. I felt like a coward, but I was relieved to be away from home at the one year mark. All in all, it was a relaxing trip. Nothing dramatic happened, which is just the way I wanted it.

By the end of May, I was still seeing my therapist, Elizabeth, but I still hadn't talked to her about some of my dark thoughts. I just talked about life in general and my "symptoms" of stress. I didn't tell her that when I saw a lingerie ad, I thought about Mia's breast being cut off. I didn't tell her that when the mailman came last week, I suddenly was convinced that he was going to break into the house and kill me. I didn't tell her about the depth of my fear. I talked about being short-tempered with Brett and Kara and my frustration that I wasn't completely better.

After awhile Elizabeth started asking me about my thoughts on Gary Mortenson. Interestingly, I didn't say I hated him and wanted him to die a slow and painful death. I wonder now if I knew what I was going to do, even then. I talked about how I thought I needed to forgive him and move on. I even talked about the bible telling us to pray for our enemies. I told Elizabeth that I wasn't there yet, but that as a Christian I hoped to one day be able to pray for Mortenson. Even as I said it, I shuddered inwardly. Of course I had no intention of ever praying for Mortenson, unless it was a prayer for God to send him straight to Hell. But I wanted Elizabeth to see me as a mentally healthy, nice person. I wasn't consciously trying to trick her. But I thought that if I acted "healthy," I would become healthy. For whatever reason, Elizabeth seemed to buy it. I didn't detect any doubt on her face or in her comments. And I actually thought I sounded pretty believable. Just a nice woman, wanting to move on and leave God to act as judge.

But I was angry, and I finally realized that I was angry at myself. I knew I was starting to think like a crazy person. I was tired of being scared. I was tired of waiting to be a victim. When I told Elizabeth that I wanted to forgive Mortenson, I thought I might actually want to do that. But after I uttered the words, I realized that was the opposite of what I wanted to do.

That was my epiphany. I wanted revenge. I wanted

Mortenson dead. And I wanted to be the one to kill him. At the time, I thought it was good that I had recognized that. I had no intention of taking any action, but I thought it was good and healthy for me to realize my true heart's desire. I was also smart enough to decide not to share that with anyone.

Slowly, during my daily meditation, I changed my imagery. I started picturing Mortenson dying. I started picturing me shooting Mortenson at close range. I started picturing him bleeding, suffering as he died. And it felt good.

At first, I was amused at this change in my imagery during meditation. I figured it probably wasn't really good to picture committing a murder while meditating. And I laughed inwardly that it made me feel better regardless. "Well," I thought. "Whatever works."

But then something interesting happened. I started sleeping. The whole night through. I started feeling, at times, actually happy. I started feeling less afraid. And feeling better opened up more time for me to think. I could concentrate on other things. And what I started thinking about, for the first time really, was the fact that Mortenson had gotten away with murdering my sister. I started thinking, for the first time, about how dangerous Mortenson continued to be. I started thinking about revenge, and about killing him. But still, it was a daydream, a fantasy of vengeance. I was an office manager for a pediatrician. I had a kindergartener. I wasn't a killer, or even a hit-man employer. Killing was wrong. God would judge Mortenson. My job was to raise my daughter and live my life as best I could. It was not to kill Mortenson. I decided that I could fantasize about killing him, if it continued to help me feel better during my meditation, but that I would not ever seriously think of killing him. I laughed at myself, and wondered if I had actually been losing it for a minute there. Me, a killer? Ludicrous.

Then, on June twenty-eighth, there was a news story about Mortenson on the radio. He had been seen hanging around downtown Middleton on a Saturday afternoon. He appeared to take an interest in the stores which catered to young women in their twenties. When the management of one of the stores recognized him and asked him to leave, Mortenson smiled and said, "It's a free country." The news story showed his picture and urged young women to remain on alert. It emphasized that Mortenson was not wanted for any crime.

The story struck me like a blow to the head. Mortenson was alive and well, and apparently on the prowl. We, the public, warranted a warning to stay vigilant. I was driving home from the store when I heard the story. I stopped at the red light at Fourth and Walton. I felt sick. I had been doing so well, and I literally felt like someone had punched me in the temple. My head pounded and my stomach hurt. My eyes were swimming with tears. "Enough!" my mind screamed. I wanted to get better. I wanted to stop being angry. I wanted to kill Mortenson. I bowed my head and prayed to God. "Please, God, give me a sign."

The light turned green. I turned right. There, at Fifth and Walton, was a new billboard. The workmen were actually still there, standing back, admiring their work. It was a sports ad. "JUST DO IT!" it read. My sign.

Although I admit that I wondered briefly if I was losing my mind, my decision to kill Mortenson felt as right as any decision I had ever made. It felt as right as deciding to marry Brett had. It felt as right as deciding to get pregnant and have Kara. I knew, however, that I couldn't do anything that would take me away from my family, especially Kara. If I was going to do this, it had to be the perfect killing. I didn't want to call it murder. It would be a justifiable homicide, a capital punishment. If I had been in a philosophical debate, I would have argued that it's only a murder if you kill a human being. Mortenson wasn't human – he was a monster. I knew I was rationalizing, but I also firmly believed I was right.

I also wasn't an idiot. I knew that if I was caught, I would be charged with murder, and sent to prison. And that wasn't acceptable.

Luckily, since Brett was a bit of a true crime buff, I had picked up a little bit of information, here and there. For example, I knew that if you wanted to get away with killing someone, you could never confide in anyone. You could never tell a soul what you had done. No bragging.

I also knew that there shouldn't be a motive for you to kill the person. That one was a problem. I had a huge motive, probably the biggest of anyone except for others in my family.

Finally, I knew that scientists could find DNA on practically anything, and connect it to the person at the scene of the crime.

These were the first things I thought of. The biggest concern for me was the fact that I had an obvious motive to kill Mortenson. When he wound up dead, the police would think of me and my family. Hopefully, Mortenson had other enemies. But I realized I didn't know much about him. I did know, because Detective Walter had told me, that Mortenson had a history of crack cocaine use. And didn't drug people kill each other all the time? Hopefully, I could make it look like a drug-related murder.

Because I felt I was on a slippery moral slope, I made a promise to myself. I would not let someone else take the blame for this killing. If someone else was charged, I would come forward and confess. I wouldn't let anyone else go to prison for something I did. But my plan was for Mortenson's killing to go unsolved.

I know it's hard to imagine that a previously law-abiding, hard-working wife and mother, whose only intentional violation of the law had been an occasional speeding violation when late for work, would make a decision to kill someone. I can't explain it very well. I just felt like it was something I had to do. I knew it would be regarded as a crime, but I felt that it was the actual opposite of that. It was the right thing to do.

I actually felt a sense of relief, having made the decision. It was the age-old conflict between doing what is right, and doing what is easy. All adults know that they are rarely the same thing. The easy thing would be to let others take responsibility for stopping Mortenson. But Mia was my sister, and stopping Mortenson was my responsibility. I would do the hard thing, the right thing, and live up to my obligation. I finally felt at peace. Now I just had to work out the details.

I noted the date, an ominous one, in my memory. June twenty-eighth. The day I decided to become a killer.

**Weird** as it sounds, besides relief at having made the decision, I felt much better in every way almost immediately after making my decision to kill Mortenson. I guess I felt a new sense of purpose. I didn't feel like a victim, or a potential victim, any longer. I felt in charge. Mortenson didn't know it yet, but he needed to be afraid of me.

I was anxious to go after him, but I didn't want anything to adversely affect my family. I thought about it in the same way I would think about taking a night class at the college, or about joining a book club. I needed to fit Mortenson's death in without screwing up the family's schedule. Kara had soccer practice on Tuesdays at six, and games on Saturday mornings. Brett had poker night with the guys on Thursdays. Brett and I both had full-time jobs. And Kara was in school again in September, which would bring the usual flurry of school-related events. I knew that once Mortenson was dead, the police would check me out on some level, even if it was just a cursory check. There couldn't be a glaring change in my routine prior to his death. This gave me something to plan for.

The Fourth of July weekend marked our first family vacation since Mia's death. Brett and I both took a few days off work and went to Lake Rainier, as we usually did. We had a barbecue and fireworks on the Fourth, and then just lazed around the day afterwards. Brett took Kara out on our little boat, presumably for fishing. I sat on the porch of the cabin in my comfy chair, with my book open. But I wasn't reading. I was thinking.

I toyed with the idea of hiring someone to kill Mortenson. I figured I could pay in cash and meet in another town, in disguise. But it seemed too risky to trust some dirt-bag with my secret. After all, I had a good reason for killing Mortenson. The person I hired would just be in it for the money and he'd have no reason to be loyal. Besides if he got caught, all he would have to do describe the age and build of the woman who had hired him, and the police would question me. And to be honest, it wasn't like I had a few thousand extra dollars lying around anyway.

No, I had to do this myself. I still had more than a few doubts about my ability to follow through with my plan, but I pushed them to the back of my mind. I would remain optimistic. I was the little engine that could. I think I can. I think I can.

At least now I had made a decision. I didn't know when or where I would kill Mortenson yet, and although

I knew which town he lived in, I didn't know his home address. There were still questions I needed to answer, but there were also parts of my plan that seemed to come instinctively. Almost immediately, I decided to use a gun. For one thing, I had visualized it many times during my meditation. For another thing, I wasn't interested in spending needless hours researching how to kill him. I knew a gun would do the trick. Getting my hand on one would be the only problem, but I figured if fifteen-year-old gang members could get one, I could too.

I spent a couple hours daydreaming about possible scenarios, but didn't come up with anything concrete. Nothing in my life had prepared me for this self-assigned mission of violence. Certainly there were thousands of victims of violent crimes, not to mention their family members, who were satisfied to let the judicial system mete out punishment. Society vilified vigilante-ism. Why then did this come so naturally to me? I wondered. I wasn't second-guessing myself or soul-searching. I had made my decision to kill and was satisfied that it was the right thing to do. I was just curious. Was this the real me? Was the ability to kill an innate skill, like being good at sports? I stared out at the lake as I thought. The sun was in my eyes, and I felt warm and relaxed. I guess I dozed off, because suddenly I was talking to Mia.

The dream was of a heated discussion that she and I had during her sophomore year of college. Mia was feverishly opposed to the death penalty, and was passionately debating me in a way that only nineteen-year-old college philosophy students could.

"Kate. How can you say that? Justified? My God!" Mia paused to blink at the tears that had filled her eyes. Until I noticed her tears I had been on the verge of laughter because of her temper. I bit back a smart-aleck retort and sighed. It was one of those arguments that had started over virtually nothing. I was reading the paper, and casually mentioned the article about a serial killer in California who'd recently been arrested. I told Mia that police had caught the guy who had been killing all those prostitutes, and that the prosecutors anticipated seeking the death penalty. "Sounds like it's justified to me," I'd simply said. "The maniac deserves it." As soon as I'd said it, I'd recognized my mistake. Mia had always been opposed to the death penalty, I remembered. She and Dad had a couple heated discussions over it back when Mia was in middle school. I noticed with regret that Mia's face had turned red and that she seemed to be steeling herself for battle. Damn it, I thought. I don't have time for this right now. I was normally pretty patient with Mia since she was the youngest, but I just wasn't feeling up to a debate at the moment. I hadn't even had breakfast yet, for God's sake.

"Mia, calm down," I urged. "He is a serial killer, you know. It's kind of hard to imagine someone who deserves it more." I closed the paper and stood up to get more coffee. I turned and smiled. "Do you want some toast?" I offered.

Mia took a deep breath. She seemed to realize she

had overreacted a bit and made a visible effort to calm herself. "Okay," she conceded. "I'll take some toast. But that doesn't mean I agree that the California guy deserves death."

I sighed, "Mia..."

"No, Kate. I'm serious. I don't want to fight, so let's just drop it for now. But promise me you'll think about it. I mean, really think about it. Who are we – you, or me, or anyone – to decide who lives or dies? If killing is wrong, isn't it wrong for everyone? Even the prisons?" I opened my mouth to answer her, but she was already getting the raspberry jam from the fridge. The toast popped up, and I reached for the butter. The discussion was officially over as we delved into coffee and toast. As we sat back down at the table, I glanced at Mia's face. Remnants of tears were still evident on her lashes. Wow, I thought. She really feels strongly about this.

As I took a bite of toast I suddenly woke from my short nap. I sat up straighter in the chair and looked over at the water to locate my family. Brett had just finished tying the boat on the dock and Kara was running toward the cabin. She was holding a line with the smallest fish I had ever seen, and beaming with joy. I left all thoughts of revenge and death behind, and went to my daughter.

**That** night, Brett held me close after we had made love. "Kate, I love you so much. I'm so glad you came back to me."

"What do you mean?" I asked, although I knew.

"Things just haven't felt the same for awhile now. I know how sad you've been. It felt like you were drifting away and I couldn't bring you back, no matter how hard I tried. Now it seems... I don't know, like you're the same again. I just want you to know how happy I am and how much I love you."

"I love you too," I said, and I meant it.

As I drifted off to sleep, I thought about how things just kept getting better and better ever since I had decided to kill Mortenson. That night I slept a peaceful nine hours wrapped in my husband's arms.

After that weekend, we got back to our normal routine. I still daydreamed about killing Mortenson, but I didn't really add any details to my plan. I decided to relax and enjoy these last summer nights after work with

Brett and Kara. It occurred to me that if something went wrong and I was caught, it might be the last summer I had with them for quite a while. I kept telling myself that wasn't an option, but I was also realistic... I knew it could happen. Strangely, that wasn't enough to give me second thoughts about following through with my plan.

Then, in late August, Kara and I were at the mall shopping for back-to-school clothes. I found myself thinking about where I could buy a gun, and realized that my idea of buying a gun as casually as I bought Kara's shoes was out of the question. Any sale would have to be in cash, since I wouldn't want anything on the credit card records and Brett would notice that kind of spending. Even if I lied to Brett about what I bought, he would remember later that I bought something expensive, and then if the police asked... We weren't poor, but we did have a budget, and a spontaneous purchase of a two or three-hundred dollar item would definitely be out of character for me.

I also didn't want a record of the purchase. I knew gun shops needed picture IDs and without a disguise or a fake license I was out of luck. There was really only one other option. If I didn't buy a gun, I would have to steal one.

Almost immediately I thought of our neighbor, Jack Blake, who was a hunting enthusiast. He was a nice guy, and Brett and I had talked with him and his wife a couple times. Jack liked to talk about his various rifles and the best weapons he used to hunt certain prey. I always smiled politely and zoned out. Normally I wasn't interested in hearing how he tracked and killed Bambi. But I knew that Jack had at least three or four guns, and he kept them in a cabinet in the middle of his living room. I didn't know if he had more in other rooms of his house, but I suspected he did.

As innocently as I could, I told Brett that we should have a barbecue sometime before the end of summer. Brett was thrilled because that was something I would have suggested back in the days when life was normal. I felt bad manipulating him, but I told myself it was for the greater good. Besides, I had my decision to kill Mortenson to thank for the improvement in my mood. I was feeling more like myself every day. I truly believed that the act of killing Mortenson, in addition to ridding the world of a real threat, would be the final step in the healing process for me. Maybe some, or even most people, could get to the acceptance stage of the grieving process without revenge coming into play. But I needed to rid the world of this monster. I don't know if I was working toward getting back to my old self, or to a new self, but I knew that I needed to kill Mortenson first. Only then would I know peace.

I told Brett that I thought we should invite more people than we normally would because our neighbors had been so helpful to us over the past year. He agreed and we decided to invite everyone on our block, plus our close friends. We planned for the last Saturday in August, and I made up little invitations on the computer that Kara and I slipped inside our neighbors' mailboxes.

I also called Lisa, who excitedly flew in from a private cruise to be there the night before so that she could help me set up. Unfortunately, the first thing she helped me with was a hangover. The night she got there we stayed up late, talking and drinking wine. But a little girl talk and wine was just what the doctor ordered. Plus, Lisa was in her nurturer's mode, and wanted to make sure I was doing better.

"Kate, you mean to tell me that you've cut down to once-a-month therapy? That could mean disaster. I mean, you're looking marvelous, but I'm sure you owe your progress to Elizabeth. You could easily back-slide into depression."

I wisely didn't argue. Instead, I changed the subject. "Speaking of looking marvelous, have you lost weight?"

"Nice try, Katie. I know you too well to fall for that. You're the one who's lost weight. You look beautiful, but I know that it's stress-related weight loss. Tell me the truth, are you sleeping?"

"I promise you, I'm sleeping. I'm doing much better. I don't go see Elizabeth very often, but she taught me some meditation and positive imagery techniques that I use all the time. It's very helpful." THIS was the right thing to say. I had embraced meditation. I knew Lisa would approve.

Lisa clapped her hands together. "I knew it! I knew that imagery would help you! What do you use?" She went on excitedly, not waiting for an answer. "I mean, I know that it might be personal. But you can tell ME!

Most people picture a soothing nature scene. What about you?" I nodded and opened my mouth to speak, but missed my chance.

"Wait, I'll tell you mine first!" Lisa lowered her voice to a conspiratorial whisper. "Well, it changed. I started off picturing myself lying on a tropical beach, with the waves licking at my feet. That was really relaxing. I loved it, I really did. Then, somehow, on its own, and I SWEAR I didn't plan it, it just kind of, you know, evolved."

I actually did know what she meant. My first fantasies of killing Mortensen had come to me in the same way: unbidden. In my more reflective moments, I had considered the fact that my subconscious knew what I needed, and had provided it to me.

I didn't tell her this, though. "What do you mean, 'evolved?'" I asked.

Lisa leaned in closer. She had a naughty look on her face that was a combination of a sweet little girl with her hand caught in the cookie jar, and a wanton vixen.

"Well," she giggled, "remember I didn't plan it, but somehow a beautiful island man entered the scene. And let's just say, the waves are no longer the only things licking at my feet!"

I laughed, truly and pleasantly surprised, although I should have known. I feigned shock, and gasped. "Lisa!"

"I know! I couldn't believe it, either! And I can't tell you how much happier I feel now after my meditation!" Lisa giggled, then whispered, "Whatever your scenario, add a man to it. It's a little known secret. It'll wake you up, start the day right." She elbowed me lightly in the ribs and added, "You know, get the ol' juices flowing."

And so on it went, until my eyes were closing and I had to go to bed. I knew I was going to look tired and pale, and would have a wine-induced headache the next morning, but it was worth it to have Lisa here. I couldn't tell her that I had planned the barbecue to gather information about guns from my neighbor, but I felt good knowing she was there with me. I wouldn't tell her what I was going to do, but I knew that if I did, she would support me to the end. Mia was my only blood sister, but Lisa was my heart sister.

The next day dawned beautiful and the forecast was a high of eighty-two degrees. After numerous cups of coffee, two Advil, and some toast, I was ready to enjoy it.

By one o'clock Brett had stocked the coolers with beer and pop, and we had the sprinkler set up so the kids could run through it. We also had a croquet course set up, as well as lawn darts, for those who wanted to play. There was a pre-season football game on, and Brett left the door to the garage open so that whoever wanted to could wander in and catch the score. I imagined that most of the men would just flat out end up in the house watching the game, but that was fine with me. I was happy to sit in the sun, talk with friends, and watch the kids play. Brett would grill the meat, because I had done most everything else. We had fruit salad, potato salad, pasta salad, chips, brownies, cookies and cake. Most of the neighbors arrived with a contribution as well, so we were in food heaven.

Kara kept dragging Lisa around by the hand, showing her this and that, and exclaiming, "Watch me!" as she jumped through the sprinkler. I was especially relieved when Jack and his wife Marta showed up. I had expected them, but I was a little nervous that they might not show. It was turning into a great day.

Still I was a little surprised, although not unhappy, to realize that I was EXCITED at the prospect of getting information from Jack. I took that as one more sign that I was doing the right thing. I felt happy about starting my plan. I knew I couldn't just bring up guns or hunting, but also I knew from past experience that Jack was a talker, and that he was his own favorite subject. I figured that all I would have to do was say "hello" and I would start hearing about Jack the great hunter.

In the end, I had to wait until after the football game was over and the grilling had started before I had an opening to talk to Jack. I had walked around, making sure that our guests all had what they needed and knew where the additional drinks were. Then I stood next to the grill, where luckily, Jack was giving Brett advice on grilling.

"Hey, Jack," I said, nonchalantly. Pleased with my brilliant opening, I continued. "Do you do much grilling?" I saw Jack's face light up. I hoped I had struck gold.

"Well, Kate, I don't grill much beef. But you know, I provide a lot of my own meat, and I like to cook that up."

"Oh, that's right, you do some hunting?"

"Right you are, Kate. Have you ever tasted grilled venison? It's delicious. And it's satisfying to know that you killed, cleaned and cooked your meal yourself, know what I mean?"

"Actually, I've never done that. I wouldn't even know where to buy venison."

"Kate! You don't BUY venison. You track it and hunt it. Fall is hunting season. If you'd like, I could take you and Brett up to Cougar Mountain and show you the ropes this year. Of course, you probably wouldn't get anything your first time, but you could learn a bit about it."

I didn't answer directly, afraid of ending the conversation. "Cougar Mountain? I didn't know that's where you hunted. Do you go to a certain town, or just walk around in the woods?"

"Well, there are some cabins at Roland on the east side. My buddies and I usually stay there. During the day we drive out to the woods and then hike in farther to do our hunting. Then at night we head back to Roland. Not much in that town except for the cabins, a pizza shop and about ten taverns!" Jack roared with laughter, apparently happy at the memory of drunken nights in Roland. "Nothing to do up there BUT hunt. If you decide to check it out, wear orange. Nobody up there but hunters, and you wouldn't want to walk around without some bright coloring."

"Oh, I don't think I could shoot a gun. Do you use one of those big ones, like the police carry?" I hoped that my dumb brunette routine wasn't arousing my husband's suspicions. I glanced at him, only to see him concentrating fully on correctly seasoning Jack's steak.

"Man, Kate, you really DON'T know much about guns. Well, sure, I bring my Glock with me for personal protection. You never know when you might run into those guys from Deliverance!" He guffawed, having cracked himself up, yet again. "But you hunt using a rifle, not a handgun. Remember, handguns are for two-legged animals!" More uproarious laughter. "That's 'people' Kate! Get it?"

Hilarious, I thought wryly. I had no idea that Jack had such a sense of humor.

"Got it," I said, smiling. "Rifles for four-legged animals, handguns for two –legged animals."

"See, you're a fast learner. You and Brett gotta check it out sometime. Although maybe you might want to stay home with Marta. She never did catch on about hunting."

I smiled to myself. I was sure that Marta, who was a dentist, could have easily "caught on" to hunting, had she wanted to. I felt a stab of compassion for poor Marta, for having to put up with Jack. She had recently mentioned to me that they were planning on starting a family soon. Maybe that would mellow out the Great Hunter.

Having lost interest in me, Jack turned his full attention to Brett, who, to my knowledge, didn't have the slightest interest in hunting. "Brett, you should try it. Nothing like it in the world. Get a couple good buddies, head up for the weekend. End the day at Ralph's Bar and Grill with a few pitchers of beer, your friends, and the knowledge that you've provided meat for the family with your own two hands. What'dya say? Join me this time?"

Brett smiled with what I recognized as his "What a nut!" smile. "Thanks Jack, but I think I'll pass. You know I fish once in awhile, but hunting's just not my thing."

"Okay, but that's too bad. In a month or two you could be grilling up some tasty venison for your family. Anyway, let me know if you change your mind. Open invitation. Now if you'll excuse me, I've gotta go sample some of that delicious potato salad."

I was thrilled. Ralph's Bar and Grill. Roland, Washington. Where men hung out and drank.

After that, any planning took the backseat to my hostess duties for the rest of the day. Which was fine by me. It was a beautiful day, and I had made a bit of progress. Why not enjoy my family and friends? I poured myself a glass of wine (hangover be damned!) and grabbed a handful of tortilla chips. I felt happy, and hopeful. That, in itself, was a reason to celebrate.

**In** early October, I had a
few minutes alone while I waited for Kara to be picked
up by her friend Dori's mom for a birthday party. I sat
in the living room so that I could see them pull up and
I switched on the TV. There was nothing on, of course,
because it was a late Sunday morning. When I got to the
local public station there was a special on outdoor sports.
I was about to change the channel, to either music vid-
eos, or the sappy women's movie channel, when the an-
nouncer spoke. "Up next, strategies to get the most out
of our local hunting season."

"Well," I thought. "Fate lends a hand."

I hadn't thought about my plan in awhile, but as I
watched the show, ideas started to form in my head. I
knew the first step was to concoct a story for Brett. After
my talk with Jack I was sure there would be some way
to get access to a gun if I could anonymously slip into a
group of hunters, but the more I thought about it, the
more I worried about trying anything close to home.

What if I saw someone I knew up toward Cougar Mountain? Then I had a great idea. Oregon! And Christmas!

A couple nights later, after dinner, I talked to Brett. "Honey, you know how I always say that I'm going to get my Christmas shopping done early, and then I never do?" My husband looked at me warily as if this was some kind of trick and I felt sorry for him. "Uh-huh?" he answered tentatively.

"Well, Oregon doesn't have a state sales tax. Lots of people drive down there to do their shopping. It would be a long drive, but with tax here at practically ten percent, it might be worth it. What do you think?"

Brett brightened. He loved to pinch pennies. "It might be fun. We could spend the day and maybe the night. Kara would love it."

"Yeah, honey, it would be fun to all go together, but Kara would get whiny after a few hours and I wouldn't be able to make any headway. I was thinking that maybe Mom and I could drive down and spend the day, maybe even stay overnight. What do you think?"

Brett looked thoughtful. "Well, if that's what you want to do. Maybe Kara and I could go to that princess movie she's been wanting to see. Are you sure you want to drive all that way just to shop?"

"Normally, no. But someone was telling me that they have great sales down there around the holidays to draw people across the border, and we could really save a bundle. Plus it might be nice to get away, just Mom and me."

"Sounds fine with me, if that's what you want. When would you go?"

"I was thinking about the Saturday after Halloween."

Brett agreed and I had no intention of asking Mom to go. Now all I had to do was steal a gun AND get my shopping done, or at least put quite a dent in it. I laughed to myself. Moral issues aside, I thought, no wonder more working moms don't commit murder. It's so hard to fit in! I played up the fact that, although it was a pain, I was looking forward to getting all my shopping done in one day. Brett was fine with it. He wasn't worried about me making a four hour drive each way, even after I told him at the last minute that Mom didn't feel up to going with me. He offered once more to go down with me instead, but I knew by now that he wanted to watch the Husky football game on Saturday, and he didn't argue when I said no.

That weekend I got up early Saturday morning and was out the door by six a.m. I knew I had a four-hour drive to the mall in Portland and I needed to get all my shopping done first so I could cover my tracks and concentrate on my real reason for being there. On my way out, I reminded Brett that if I was too tired, I would stay over in a motel. I told him I didn't want to risk driving while I was too sleepy. He agreed that was best, and I said I'd call him with an update around dinner time.

There wasn't much traffic, and I got to the mall a little after ten. I actually began to get into the spirit of

Christmas while I shopped. Most of the stores had decorated for Christmas immediately after Halloween, so the mall looked fairly festive. There were even Christmas carols piped into a few of the stores. I surprised myself by humming along with "Deck the Halls" and "Jingle Bells." I wondered if there was some kind of subliminal message in the background whispering "Buy more!" But for whatever reason, I was enjoying myself.

One of my last stops was the electronics store, where I picked up some DVDs and CDs for Brett, Kara, and Mom. I was even able to order a few things for Robert and his family and get them shipped directly to his home. After that I moved on to some specialty stores within the mall. Unexpectedly I found a beautiful picture frame. It was perfect for a picture I had of Robert, Mia, and me. I bought three of the frames and thought I would get prints made for Robert and Mom for Christmas. Then we would all have them in matching frames. I tried not to think about the fact that there should have been a fourth one too. Mia's.

On the way out I saw a kiosk that had several maps for sale and I purchased an Oregon map. The teenager who sold it didn't look up from his text-messaging, other than to scan the bar-code on the map, announce the price, and hand it back to me. I felt good about that. The mall was packed, and I was dressed like just about every other woman there. T-shirt, jeans, winter jacket. I didn't think that buying a map would cause any suspicions later, but even if it did, I doubted the clerk would remember anything about me. I paid in cash, just to be sure.

My final destination was a large toy store. I had purposely saved it for last, because I tended to go overboard with Kara. I thought that if I was really tired, and somewhat broke, that I would be able to control myself. As if. Before I left the toy store, I bought a short, curly brown wig in the dress-up aisle. It was a spur of the moment decision. I didn't have a chance to try on the wig, but if it fit, and looked decently real, I figured I would wear it that night. In the dark, it would at least make me look different. Different was good.

I left the mall and drove south on Interstate Five, passing several billboards that proclaimed ample lodging and "good eats" for hunters in a town called Warrenville. I paid attention to the signs as I left the freeway and headed towards town. After I had driven awhile longer, I stopped and studied the map. Warrenville was still about eighty-five miles east, and a bit south of my location. It was a small dot on the map, and I assumed it wasn't a major town. It looked perfect.

Before I started the car again I grabbed some black duct tape from the backseat. I had taken it from the work bench at home before leaving. I hadn't taken the whole roll, on the off chance that Brett would need it, but I was a little worried about having Washington license plates in Oregon. I had seen tons of Washington vehicles at the mall, and I knew that Washington plates wouldn't stick out like Texas plates would, but it was still something that someone might notice. I went around to the back of the car and used strips of duct tape to turn an F to an H, and an I to a T on my plates, and then did the same on the front plates. After I had gotten far enough away, I could just strip the tape off and no one would know.

After that I drove to the next hotel I saw and got a room. I called Brett as soon as I got inside and told him I had a lot of success shopping, but that I was suddenly just worn out. I didn't think I could drive home safely. Brett said he wasn't surprised, since I had left so early. We'd been married long enough that I knew he was wondering if the savings in sales tax had just been cancelled out by the cost of the motel room, but he didn't say anything. I was always the one who planned for Christmas, and I loved it. In truth, I knew I had the easy part. Kara was a busy girl and I knew Brett hadn't been lying around all day. But I was a little tired, and Brett could hear it in my voice. He was sweet as usual, and told me he would see me the next day. He asked me to call him when I was on the road home and we said goodnight.

By then it was seven o'clock and I decided to head toward Warrenville. I tried the wig on, and it looked okay. In the dark I figured it would look even more like real hair. I put my cell phone on vibrate on the off chance Brett called back, grabbed the duct tape and the map, and went to my car.

I made good time on the drive to Warrenville. Soon enough, the signs appeared and I got the impression that the town got most of its tourism during hunting season. I saw several signs for Bob's Gun Shop and then two signs for Paul Bunyan's Pizza, Beer, and Burgers. The sign for Paul Bunyan's touted the restaurant as the "hunter's best friend" and a "local favorite." As I got within twenty miles of Warrenville, I saw a large billboard that exclaimed, "Spend your days in the woods and your nights at Paul Bunyan's." I took that as a sign (no pun intended) that there would be hunters among Paul Bunyan's clientele.

It was after eight, and it was dark. I took a side road that didn't seem to lead to anything close by, and I didn't see any houses or businesses as I pulled over to the side of the road. Looking around uneasily, I turned off the head-lights and was surprised at the complete dark of the country road. I put my wig back on without turning on the dome light. I could only see my silhouette in the rearview mirror, but at least my shadow looked natural and not lopsided. I hoped my car was invisible on the road, but not so invisible that someone would run into me if they suddenly turned down my way. There didn't seem to be many cars back on the main road however, so I got out and checked the duct tape on my license plates one more time.

It was colder than I'd expected, and I wished I'd thought to bring gloves. My stomach was getting nervous and emitted a loud growling sound. Great. I hoped I wasn't in for a bout of nervous diarrhea. I allowed myself a moment of self-pity. You never saw movie-stars chug Pepto-Bismol before walking into danger, I thought. Why couldn't anything be easy? I forced myself to take a deep breath and evaluate how I felt. I realized that I actually felt good, both mentally and physically. I was nervous, but in an excited kind of way. It was hard to explain, but after months of mourning and sadness, taking action made me feel in control. I took a moment to give myself a mental pat on the back for having successfully gotten this far. When I felt I had my head back in the game, I got back into the car. I carefully turned back towards the main road with the headlights off. I waited until no cars were visible on the main road and then turned right. I flipped my headlights on, and headed for Paul Bunyan's.

drove right by the bar, only slowing down slightly. I wanted to find a place within a short walking distance from the parking lot and I found a spot down the road a bit where five or six other cars were parked. I didn't know whether these would be hunter's cars or overflow from Paul Bunyan's, although the lot hadn't looked completely full. At any rate, I backed in so that I could drive right back onto the road. I looked at myself in the rear-view mirror, but could barely see anything because I still wasn't willing to turn the dome light on and there were no street lights.

I climbed out of the car and locked it, putting the keys in my pocket. "It's now or never," I thought, then laughed inwardly at my increasing use of clichés in everyday life.

The sky was clear and the three-quarter moon shone down brightly enough that I could see my breath and about five feet in front of me, but that was all. I felt relieved that I would be pretty much invisible while walking along the road towards Paul Bunyan's, unless a car came by. I hoped to be quick enough to avoid that, but it wasn't as if I was completely away from civilization, and I had seen three or four cars pass me as I drove to the restaurant.

I started walking toward the tavern. I was nervous, but I hoped the walk would ease my nerves. At least it wasn't raining. The air was cold and smelled pure, like it was blowing straight down off a mountain river. The crunch of gravel under my feet and the rhythm of my breath started to sound like a cadence to me. "I think I can. I think I can." I crunched my way down the road to Paul Bunyan's, hoping that I really could.

No cars passed me on my short walk, and I was happy about that. I didn't see anyone in the parking lot at Paul Bunyan's either. I knew I should be as quick as possible. I started walking slowly, and I hoped casually, toward the business. As I passed the trucks in the lot, I snuck peeks inside but I didn't see any guns. As I got closer to the tavern, I saw a green Ford pickup. It was older and a bit beat-up. I hoped that the fact that the owner was too lazy to fix the dents and the scratches in the paint, also meant that he was careless with his guns. I looked inside. Nothing. I decided to try the door and found it was unlocked. I opened the door on the passenger side and started to lean in, with the intention of looking under the seats. I was suddenly disgusted with myself that I hadn't tried the doors on the trucks that were nearer the road. When I leaned in, the seat gave a loud squeak that made my heart jump.

"Lucy, is that you?" I jumped again and turned, assuming I looked as guilty as I felt. There was a very large, very drunk forty-something-year-old man standing just behind me. "What?" I asked, frozen to the spot.

"Well hell, John never mentioned you were so pretty. I mean, he said you were pissed that he went hunting on your anniversary. We had one other wife come up to surprise her hubby with some midnight lovin' a couple years back. I bet John never thought you'd do anything like that! Wait 'til I tell him you're out here!" Then, through his drunken haze, he asked, "You ARE Lucy, right?"

I spoke without thinking and was amazed at my newfound ability to think on the fly. "Of course I'm Lucy. What the hell are you saying? Does John have a girlfriend or something?" My thoughts were racing. Should I run? Continue to lie? Why did I think I could do this? Shit!

Luckily, the big man seemed well trained not to interfere in domestic squabbles. "Oh, no, ma'am! You know, most of us have never met one another's wives. I didn't mean to say nothing about a girlfriend. I just know John felt a little bad about leaving you on your anniversary. But he thought that if he brought home a nice buck, you'd appreciate that." The man trailed off. Perhaps he realized how absurd this was.

Still he seemed to have bought my story, and he was visibly drunk, so I doubted he would ever be able to identify me. I decided to take a chance. "I just wanted to make sure that John had locked the truck and that his gun was safe. But of course, he left the truck unlocked!" I did my best to look disgusted with my fake husband.

"Well, Lucy, nothing to steal in there. You know John wouldn't leave his guns in the truck! Don't be mad at him after you came all this way to surprise him. I'll bet you've got something pretty special in mind for him, now don't cha honey?" The man stepped closer, and I was repulsed by the overwhelming scent of beer, cigarettes, and sweat that pervaded the air around his big frame. "John sure never let on that you were so pretty!" he repeated.

Since I was sickened by the man's stench of alcohol, I decided to let it show. "Well, he'd better not be as drunk as you are! And don't you dare tell him I'm out here. I want to wait in the truck and surprise him when he comes out. Now go on before you wreck the surprise!"

The man brightened. "Don't you worry! I won't tell him a thing. I'll just send him out and tell him he'd better check on his truck!"

My mind was screaming at me to run back to my car and get the hell out of there. Instead, I heard myself say, "You do that honey. Go on now."

What in the world was I thinking? As crazy as it seemed, a plan was starting to form in my mind. John's truck was about twenty feet from the trees at the edge of the parking lot, but it was still pretty close to the tavern. I decided to walk over to the tree line where I would hopefully be out of sight. Then I could wait to see what happened next, and go from there.

I waited only about four or five minutes, but it seemed like forever. My heart was pounding. I tried some deep breathing exercises, but the sound of my deep breathing, there in the woods, reminded me too much of a horror movie. I was leaning towards running away, when a short man in his late forties staggered out of the bar. He was holding two rifles under his left arm, and was fumbling with what looked like keys, with his right hand. I waited, wondering whether this was John, or some other drunken slob.

As luck would have it, the man approached John's truck. I was happy that he appeared to be even more drunk than the other guy had been. I eyed the guns he was carrying. I had hoped for a handgun, but would take a rifle if I had no other choice.

I slowly walked toward the passenger side of the truck, and got within ten feet just as John heavily lowered himself onto the driver's side seat. I wasn't sure what I was going to say. I would ask for directions, I supposed. Maybe pretend to feel sick and ask him to go get me a drink of water from the bar, then steal his guns while he was gone. Huh, I thought – it just might work!

John caught sight of me just as I got to the passenger side of his truck. I gave a little wave, and opened the passenger door, but before I could open my mouth, John let out a squeal of delight. "Ooooh-eee! Sam said there was a little something at my truck that would light my fire, and he wasn't kidding. You ARE a hot little number!"
"Huh?" I asked.

John went on, boisterous and unable to keep his happiness to himself. "The boys knew that my bitch-of-a-wife, Lucy, didn't want me to come hunting this weekend, cause it's our anniversary. Huh! She conveniently forgot about my birthday and managed to go to the spa with her girlfriends! But just the same, these guys are sure the best friends a man could have. Hiring me a little lovin' to cheer me up!"

My inability to speak remained. "He thinks I'm a hooker!" I thought. For some reason, instead of panicking, I smiled at the thought. It was a mistake. John took this as a sign that I was ready to get started. "C'mon baby! Pleasure me!" he said. To my horror, John started unzipping his jeans and touching himself. Luckily, his large belly obscured any sign of the penis I assumed must have been there somewhere.

"Get in, baby. I'm ready for you. Lucy wouldn't suck me off if her life depended on it. C'mon sweetie, I don't bite." He paused a moment and then added, "That is, unless you want me to!" John guffawed at his own feeble joke. "C'mon!"

I had no intention of touching John. I really needed to run away now. Neither my legs, nor my brain was listening, though, because instead of running, I heard myself say, "I can't get in. Nowhere to sit. The guns are in the way."

John looked over at the rifles on the seat beside him. "Go ahead and just move 'em to the floor," he said gruffly.

"I don't like guns," I lied. "I want them out of the

truck before I get in. Then you'll get your surprise." Surprise! What surprise? I smiled so he wouldn't see how anxious I was.

"Okay sweetheart. Don't worry. I know you girls have to be careful. I'll just lay 'em outside my door." John picked up the two rifles and opened his driver's side door. He bent down, laying the rifles just outside the door.

"Okay," I said. "Are those all the guns? I mean it! They all have to be out before you get your surprise." Damn it. I had gotten in over my head. Surprisingly though, I felt calmer. My heart wasn't hammering any longer. I felt in control, at least of my emotions. Clearly John was the one at the disadvantage, since he was drunk and had now considerably pulled his pants down to his upper thighs. I figured that he knew from experience that even the most talented prostitute would need all the help she could get to find his penis underneath that enormous belly. But I also figured that he wouldn't be able to run after me very well with his pants down. I felt – what's the word? – emboldened by the situation.

"Jesus Christ! I've got my handgun under the seat," John said. He sounded like he was beginning to lose his patience. "I'll put it out, too. Then that's it!" He reached under the seat and took out a black handgun. Bingo! Just what I wanted. "Now get your ass in here and start sucking, darling. I ain't in the mood for any small talk." His mood was fluctuating a bit. He had gone from happy to surly in a span of seconds. I clearly remembered why I hated to be around drunks. But then he brightened.

"Now what's my surprise? I mean, you're a nice surprise and all. But is there something else? I mean, another surprise?" He looked at me hopefully, then apparently remembered he had gone almost ten seconds without touching his dick, and started to rub it again. It reminded me of CPR or something. He was trying so hard to bring it to life.

"Mary," I said suddenly. "Mary's your surprise."

John sat up a little straighter, while my mind tried to grasp why I had just said that. I thought of a story Lisa told me once about a guy she dated who decided to share a fantasy with her. His twist on the common threesome fantasy was that he wanted one of the girls to be slutty, and the other girl to be innocent. He decided to broach the idea with Lisa on their fifth date. Lisa wasn't up for his threesome idea, but she was interested in finding out which one the guy thought SHE was, in his little virgin/whore fantasy. Unfortunately for him, he told her that he thought she would be the older, slutty one. Had he broached the subject more delicately, perhaps Lisa would have declined to participate, but forgiven him and given him another chance. However, letting her know that he saw her as both "older" and "slutty" and that he also wanted a younger and more innocent woman to join them in bed, pretty much ruined any chance of a sixth date. End of fantasy, end of date, end of relationship. Still, that's where my genius idea came from. I didn't know why I said "Mary," but I assumed that made her the innocent one. I was older, and I supposed, since I was pretending to be a hooker, already the slutty one.

John smiled. "Who's Mary? Where is she?" He looked around, as if expecting a second female to materialize out of the glove box.

"She's around the corner. You see, I've been doing this for awhile. But she's new. She's really worried that you'll be too," I paused, for dramatic affect, "well, BIG for her." John beamed, and stuck out his chest with pride. I went on. "She doesn't have much experience. She gets intimidated when we meet a man who's had a lot of women." I saw I had said the right thing, because John began stroking himself in earnest. Strangely though, and to my relief, his dick remained invisible.

"I'll just go get Mary, and we'll get started," I said, trying to sound casual. John stopped stroking. He looked at me with suspicion and a bit of sadness in his eyes. "You're not messing with me, right? I mean, the guys paid you and everything, right? You'll be back?" he asked.

Great, I thought. A guilt trip. But I worked through it in seconds. John was, of course, about to cheat on his wife. So I could justify this. Tomorrow he would be glad he'd remained true to Lucy during their anniversary weekend.

"Of course I'll be back. They only paid me half. Mary and I get the other half after you tell them we did a good job." John smiled like a fat kid with cake, which brought me a second's more guilt. "Give me a couple minutes. Like I said, Mary's shy." Then I said something that I hoped would distract him a little longer. "There's just one thing. Mary likes to start with me. She likes it when the guy watches. Then we'll do you. Is that okay?" I smiled my sexiest, and I hoped, most prostitute-like smile. John didn't answer, but moaned aloud. His hand started moving faster. Another cliché men's fantasy, but I guess I said the right thing!

"Be right back!" I shouted cheerfully. I closed the passenger door and walked quickly to the back of the truck. I looked in the driver's side mirror to see if John was looking. I couldn't see well, but he seemed occupied. The truck was actually rocking, and I thought it was a good possibility that John would supply his own happy ending to the story I had concocted at any moment. I'd better hurry.

I bent down and crept around towards the driver's side. I moved, as quietly as I could along the side of the truck. A couple times along the way, I heard a leaf crunch under my feet and I froze, waiting to hear the truck door open. But all I heard was John's quick, desperate breathing as the truck continued to vibrate. At last I made it to the driver's door. I could see a dark spot on the ground just beneath the truck. I inched forward until my hand was just within reach of its mark. I didn't dare crawl forward any more. I felt along the dirt and leaves until I felt the cold metal of the rifles. I moved my hand along the ground next to the rifles until I felt the handgun. I grabbed it and pulled it slowly toward me. It was heavier than I thought. I held it away from me, careful to keep my finger off the trigger. I crawled backward toward the rear of the truck. My heart was pounding and I couldn't hear anything but my own breathing, quick and shallow.

I crept toward the road as quickly and as quietly as I could for about thirty feet, and then broke into a run. Once I made it around the corner out of the lot, I ran as fast as I could toward my car. I prayed that I wouldn't hear John behind me. As I ran, I heard a car coming down the road. I ran into the tree line and froze. The car passed me without slowing. It was on the main road, and hadn't come from Paul Bunyan's. I started running again, and didn't stop until I'd gotten to my car. There were still a couple cars in the area where I'd parked, but they didn't look occupied. I unlocked my door and got in, putting the gun under the driver's seat. I was breathing hard and I could still feel my heart pounding, but I forced myself to pull out of the dirt lot at a casual speed. On the main road I was careful to drive the speed limit although I wanted to floor it.

When I got about five miles down the road, I pulled over. It was still very dark, and there were no street lights. I got out of the car, and quickly pulled the duct tape off of both license plates. I kept the duct tape in the car. I wasn't sure if the police could get prints or DNA from duct tape, but I didn't want to leave it near where I'd stolen the gun. I thought I should ditch the wig at some point, too. But there were lots of garbage cans between there and Washington State. I'd clean out the car on the way home. I might be a thief and pretend prostitute, but

I was no litter-bug.

I couldn't believe it. I'd done it and gotten away! As I drove, I found myself smiling and giggling at times. I knew that was inappropriate. One's first felony should be a somber occasion, but I couldn't help it. I was so relieved!

I made it back to my motel room in time for the eleven o'clock news. I looked at the stolen gun, which I'd brought with me into the room. It looked well cared for. I didn't know much about guns, but I knew that the clip went into the gun like the candy went into a Pez dispenser. I played around until I was able to get the clip out. It was full of bullets. I put the clip back in, and felt it lock into place before I put the gun in my purse and lay down on the bed. My nerves kicked in then, and suddenly I started crying. But it was relief crying, not sad crying. I had done it! It was scary, but I had done it. John would never be able to identify me, and the other guy thought I was John's wife. I had gotten away with it! I felt, I don't know, victorious, and proud of myself. I suddenly had the urge to call Lisa and tell her how she had inspired me with her threesome story. But I knew I could never tell anyone anything about what I'd done. Still, I'd achieved my goal. And I had gotten the Christmas shopping done at a discount. Life was good. I fell into a deep sleep, and didn't wake until the sun peered in through the curtains. I took a long, hot shower, grabbed the free continental breakfast and was on the road home by ten.

I got home early in the afternoon. After hugs and

kisses, I made Kara and Brett leave the room so that I could unload the presents from the trunk. I hid them in the same storage closet where I hid the presents every year. I also put the gun in my sewing kit on a shelf in the back of the closet. Brett never went in that closet and I didn't sew, except to replace a button or occasionally mend a tear. I knew the gun was safe in there.

After that, I heard all about the new princess movie that Brett and Kara had seen the night before. By then it was almost dinner time. Brett suggested we go out to dinner, since neither of us was in the mood to cook. We settled on an Italian place we like called Michaelangelos. Everything felt like normal and after a nice dinner at Michaelangelos we were home by six-thirty. Kara went to bed a little late, and Brett and I watched Law and Order on TV together before calling it a day. Cuddling close in bed, my activities from the night before seemed like a dream. But I knew that the Glock forty caliber handgun sat in my sewing kit, waiting for me to take the next step.

# Thanksgiving

came and went and things were good. Brett wasn't mad about the money I'd spent on Christmas gifts. I think he was just so happy to have his "old" wife back. I actually felt pretty good, although I'd be lying if I said I didn't have bad days. In fact, there were days when I missed Mia so much that I thought I would die myself.

One day in particular it hit me again. Brett had watched a show while I sat at the coffee table working on our Christmas cards. An hour later he started snoring loudly and I woke him up and asked him to go to bed. I was almost done with the cards, but I was losing my interest in them. I decided to look for something festive on TV to keep me motivated. I started flipping channels without a planned destination. It was rare for me to start watching a show that late at night, and I had no idea what was on. I was pleasantly surprised to find that Gone With The Wind was on Channel forty-five! I hadn't seen it in years. Mia and I always watched it together when she was a teenager. She used to tease me that I was the only person who rooted for Melanie more than for Scarlett. The truth was that I identified with Melanie more than Scarlett. Mia, however, was always a staunch defender of everything that Scarlett did. She loved Scarlett's strength, determination, and survival skills. I thought Scarlett was a bitch. At any rate, Mia and I would make big bowls of popcorn and cuddle on the couch and watch the movie whenever we realized it was on. It was a private thing just between the two of us.

That night when I saw that Rhett and Scarlett were on TV again, I smiled. Mia would love this! I put down my cards and pen, and without thinking, picked up the phone. I had the first three digits of my sister's cell phone number entered, when I remembered she was dead. Suddenly I couldn't breathe. In a panic I stood up, and then my knees buckled and I fell to the floor. Once there, I found I could breathe again, but like a swimmer too long in the water, felt too weak and heavy to climb back up. I remained there on the floor, the weight of my sorrow immobilizing me.

Episodes like that had struck me several times. There were lots of things in daily life that reminded me of Mia, like seeing that her favorite soup was the special at a diner, or that her favorite perfume was on sale, and those small things always sent a quick stab of pain through my heart.

Life went on. Funny how that happens. I got my cards done two nights later, and Christmas rushed towards us. Brett loved his gift certificate to the Golf Pro Shop, and

Kara loved all her gifts, especially the princess-themed ones. We had a good day. Time passed quickly and it was suddenly New Year's Eve. We stayed home for the second year in a row and had Mom over for dinner. We agreed that we would have a quiet celebration and that Mom would spend the night, rather than driving out amongst the drunks. It was nice. Kara ran around, eating chips and dip and watching TV specials with Brett. Mom and I sat in the kitchen, not exactly sad, but subdued, nevertheless. Neither of us said what both of us were thinking in our own way – that a New Year was upon us, but Mia was still dead, and her killer still free and unpunished. Instead, Mom started talking about happy times with Mia. Things that made us both smile and laugh.

"Mom, how do you do it? How do you stay so strong?" I asked.

"Well sweetie, you know, after your dad died, I thought I would die too. I thought there could be nothing worse. And then Mia died." She paused and swallowed, but then she smiled. "And I found out that there WERE worse things. But God brought us through and we're doing okay. I just have to trust in God that he has a plan. That's really all I can do."

"No, Mom, I mean, how do you keep your emotions so under control? I feel like I have to keep a tight rein on my emotions or they'll take me over. But you're so open, without being a mess. How do you manage?"

"Well, hon, I'll tell you. I think the key is to keep letting the tears out a little at a time. When you hold it in, it's only a matter of time before you blow. Just cry when you feel like crying, and laugh when you feel like laughing. No bottling up. If I have a secret, I guess that's it. That, and country music."

I laughed. "Okay, now you've lost me."

"Well," Mom said, "Have you ever listened to country music? Every other song is about death and heartbreak. I listen to country music in the car while I'm running my errands, and those songs make me cry every day. No chance of any tears piling up inside, as long as I've got Creekside Country on the dial. That, and the Women's Movie channel."

"Mom, you crack me up. Why didn't you tell me this before I spent all that time and money in counseling?"

Mom reached over and squeezed my hand, letting me know that she understood I was only half-joking. She was a little old-fashioned about the whole counseling thing, but she knew I'd had a hard time, and was glad that seeing someone had helped. But then she changed the subject to the upcoming after-Christmas sales, which is pretty much as I'd expected. The conversation we'd just had was about as detailed as Mom ever got in talking about her feelings. She was raised to keep one's innermost feelings private. I knew my Mom would do anything in the world for me, but she'd also never discuss the depth of her feelings. So I was content to talk about the slashed prices on holiday items at the department stores that week instead.

The truth was that I was doing pretty well emotionally. I continued my counseling with Elizabeth because I was afraid to take a step backwards though. The bad times still really hurt when they materialized, but they came less often. And I continued to sleep pretty well. I had even gained some of the weight back that I'd lost, and I was feeling pretty decent.

The other reason I kept going to counseling though was for future defense issues. Once I had killed Mortenson, I wanted to make sure there was a counselor who could say that I was reacting appropriately to my grief issues. I was careful to talk about how my main goal was to let go of the anger and move past thinking about Mortenson. I usually just talked with Elizabeth about daily life – juggling work with being a mom and wife – but we also talked about my feelings about Mia a lot. I was only seeing Elizabeth once a month now, which she said was healthy. She said that I was working towards the last step of grief – acceptance – but that I wasn't there yet. So I continued to see her, and worked on appearing gentle and sweet and very un-felon-like. It seemed to be working. I had a genuine affection for Elizabeth, and I felt that she liked me and trusted that I was being honest. Normally, I would have felt bad for deceiving her, but she was charging quite a bit of money per hour, and I felt like she was being adequately reimbursed for our time together. She was a professional after all, and she was really helping me. It was still nice to talk about Mia and how much I missed her, and to keep those feelings from piling up. And I was aware that it wouldn't have been fair to Elizabeth to involve her in any future police investigation by disclosing to her my thoughts of murder. No, it was better to let her believe what I showed her – a grief-stricken sister, who was slowly getting back on her feet, and who wouldn't, and couldn't, hurt a fly.

A big part of my plan to kill Gary Mortenson relied on my ability to keep tabs on him without raising any suspicion, and it was Lisa who unexpectedly provided me with that information. After Mortenson had been released, she had somehow obtained Mortenson's exact address, work address, work hours, and vehicle information. I knew that Lisa routinely did background checks on potential employees and potential boyfriends through a private detective agency, and I assumed that she had used this resource. By nature, Lisa was pretty trusting, but she had gotten burned a bit when she first inherited her millions. Unfortunately for Lisa, she found out that there were people out there who wanted to spend time with her just because she was a millionaire. Pretty basic for the rest of us, but it was news to Lisa. Once bitten, twice shy, and she began to use her detective agency as needed.

Lisa had handed me a sheet of paper that provided me all of Mortenson's information a few months ago. I insisted I didn't need it, but put it in a drawer. Based on the reports she had gathered Mortenson was still working construction for Work First Construction in Belmont, and was still living at the Mary Louise apartments in downtown Belmont. Lisa told me not to worry, she would check on Mortenson monthly, and she would immediately report any change to me.

In February I decided I had better act. I either had to shoot Mortenson before, or after, April. I didn't want to kill him anywhere near Mia's anniversary date. I had intentionally taken my time with this, but I was getting the feeling that time was running out. I didn't know why I felt this way, whether it was intuition, or just a feeling that my luck might run out. But I felt sure that something was going to change. I was starting to worry that I was going to miss my chance.

I joined an aerobics class at the YMCA because I needed a reason to be out of the house at night at least a couple times a week. I scheduled the class for seven p.m. It was a one hour class, but I told Brett that I might want to either swim, or use the sauna, after class, so that he should figure I'd be gone on those nights from six-thirty until ten p.m. I felt bad, because that put me out of the house at Kara's bed time, but it was only an eight week class. I told Brett that I wanted to get in shape for summer, and that once it started staying lighter in the evenings, that I would just be able to run after dinner, and I wouldn't have to go to the gym. Brett knew that I didn't feel safe going running or walking alone after dark. He wasn't thrilled that I would be gone three nights a week, but lately Brett had been pretty engrossed in a TV series that I had been giving him a hard time about. With the thought of having the television to himself most nights, he readily agreed to my new schedule.

My plan was to give myself time to drive to Belmont, kill Mortenson, and get back home before anyone missed me. I knew I had to start a routine that would allow me to do that. So I started hanging out at the YMCA after my class was finished. I usually walked around the track for a bit, then sat in the sauna, then showered and went home.

After the first couple of classes I told Brett that I might be home a bit late because I was going to do the grocery shopping after class either on Mondays or Wednesdays. Sure I was tired, but I told him it was worth it to go when the store wasn't crowded. It was typical for me to try and be efficient with my time, so he didn't think much about it. That night I skipped the walking and the sauna after my aerobics class and drove over to Belmont, just to time the drive. I was pleased to see that it was fairly close. I also guessed that Mortenson probably got the apartment after he had been hired at the Work First Construction Company, because his apartment and construction company were only about five miles apart.

I listened to the classic rock station on the way, because listening to songs from when I was in high school always brought back good memories. I wanted to keep my confidence up. This was just a little re-con mission. "No need to be nervous," I told myself. I tried to tell myself that the trickle of sweat in the small of my back was a by-product of my earlier aerobics class, and that the tightness in my gut was from skipping dinner.

I arrived in Belmont and easily found Mortenson's

neighborhood. As I approached, a fluffy white cat darted into the road and ran into the shrubbery. I took it as a positive sign, kind of the opposite of a black cat crossing my path. I drove past Mortenson's apartment building and was pleased that there were no pedestrians in the area. I was also happy to see that his unit was a ground floor apartment, and that it had an assigned parking spot that was visible from the street. There was no vehicle in the spot, and I hoped that meant that Mortenson wasn't home. Lisa's information had included Mortenson's car's make and model and his license plate number and I saw nothing that fit that description.

After driving by his apartment, I got back on the freeway and headed back to Middleton. It was after nine when I got back. I went to the store and bought the groceries, and was back home by ten-thirty. Brett didn't bat an eye, and I felt like things had gone well.

I knew that if I became a suspect in Mortenson's murder, the police would check to see if I'd been to aerobics as usual on the night of the murder. I would need to go to class and do everything as normal that night, so that nothing seemed different. I also planned to run some errands afterwards, to explain any delay in getting home. I wasn't worried about anyone checking my mileage. Brett and I both commuted a good bit to and from work and tended to use a lot of gas.

I thought I had been prepared to kill Mortenson, but I realized that it had seemed a far-off daydream-type goal before this. Now I started to think about doing it in the same way I would think about any other chore. It was inevitable, and it had to be done. By the third week of aerobics class I had driven to Belmont after class twice. The second time I went there, I actually saw Mortenson pull into his parking space at his apartment. Luckily, it was dark and I had pulled to the curb across the street. He never looked in my direction, and I didn't think he saw me at all. Even so, my heart was pounding and I could feel the thin sheen of sweat at my hairline. Just the sight of Mortenson made me feel a little nauseous. This was the last person Mia had ever seen on earth. I had only seen him briefly on the news and in the courtroom long ago, but I instantly recognized him. From only a few feet away his appearance terrified me in a different way than it had when I saw him in police custody. Up close and in the middle of his daily routine he looked like a normal blue-collar construction worker, and not in the least threatening. He looked like the kind of guy you would have a conversation with if he asked how you were doing. How would anyone ever see death coming when it looked like him? I felt my breath quicken and I got a little dizzy as gooseflesh broke out along my arms. I forced myself to focus and to breathe deeply and slowly. "Focus!" I screamed inwardly. I noted that it was four after nine. Mortenson was carrying a twelve pack of beer under his left arm, and a sack that said "Rainy's" on it with his right. I was familiar with the Rainy's grocery chain. I wanted to remember this information. It might come in handy.

I watched Mortenson enter unit number eight, and then I drove away. I was feeling calmer, and although I was a little disappointed that I had gotten scared when I saw him, I reminded myself that I hadn't backed down or fled. I had stayed and gathered some information. Not much, but I forced myself to look at the bright side. "I can do this!" I thought. I had no one to encourage me, so I had to encourage myself. Self-confidence was at least half the battle.

I got back to Middleton and to the grocery store. There seemed to be a steady stream of customers no matter what time I went to the store, but it was still markedly less crowded than it would have been earlier in the evening. I thought that if the police asked, someone would remember me. Plus I always used my grocery discount card and paid with my debit, so I needed to continue to do that. I knew that they could easily verify what time I got there, and even what I had purchased. I tried to be careful to act normal at the store. This was actually easy, because the act of grocery shopping itself was so tiresome and mundane that I felt myself calming almost as soon as I wheeled the cart down the produce aisle.

But that night, I couldn't sleep. I felt like I was missing something. Surely there would be suspicions about my timing if I was considered as a suspect. All the detectives would have to do was see what time I had left the YMCA, and what time I had bought the groceries, in order to work out a timeline. The drive to Belmont was what was killing me. I was going to lose a little over an hour. How could I explain that? I didn't know, but I had better figure it out, and soon.

On the Wednesday of my fifth week of aerobics class, I had an idea. Shopping was an excuse that had served me well when I got the gun, and I had already established that I was in the habit of running errands after aerobics. What if I went to the mall to shop after working out? I had started going out the back door of the YMCA after my sauna time, and I was pretty sure that the staff wouldn't be able to pinpoint when I left. When I arrived at the mall I could park around the side and enter through one of the smaller stores. I thought it was likely the mall had video-surveillance at the main entrance, and inside the mall, but I doubted they had them at the smaller store entrances. And it would be dark, so maybe they wouldn't be able to see me clearly anyway. I could work out, kill Mortenson, and then go to the mall. And since the mall was only twenty minutes north of Belmont, I could get there quickly afterwards. If asked, I would just have to be vague about the time I got to the mall. I would need to give myself a thirty minute window and give a range of time that would overlap my time in Belmont. Plus the mall was open until eleven p.m. every night except Sundays.

"Mortenson", I thought, "You're a dead man." Then I chuckled. "God, I've got to stop watching bad TV shows with Brett," I thought. Even my thoughts were starting to sound clichéd. But I was happy. I was closer to completing the plan. And my butt had already gotten visibly firmer from aerobics class.

Work was crazy for the next few days and I didn't have any more time to think seriously about Mortenson for the remainder of the week, although by now he was always at the back of my mind, like a chore that I had postponed. I was well aware that the clock was ticking. I had to move fast.

14

still felt like I needed some more information about Mortenson, but time was running out. I had gone to his home only twice more in the previous weeks. Once he was home, and once he had just been pulling up when I got there. I decided to go back out on Monday, and on Wednesday during the week of March eighteenth. I would take the gun both times, in case an opportunity presented itself. That meant I had a week to think through the details of my plan.

By the next day I was starting to feel nervous. I hoped it was nerves, and not the flu, but my stomach was in knots. I realized I hadn't given much thought to what I would do with the gun after I shot Mortenson. Obviously, I would have to get rid of it. But where?

I forced myself to calm down and think. This was not that hard. People shot one another all the time. The main reason they were caught was because of the tie they held to the victim, and the physical evidence left behind. But I figured there was a way around these obstacles. There had to be. Strange as it may seem, I felt I had "right" on my side. I felt that I would get away with this. I wouldn't allow myself to think about the possibility of getting caught. I thought of a parallel to mountain climbing. When you reach the top, you are only half-way done, because you must safely descend the mountain. Killing Mortenson would be only half my journey. I had to keep from being caught.

I decided that I should hedge my bets a bit, and wear a disguise to the scene. One night I left for aerobics about thirty minutes early and went to Toby's Thrift Store. I bought multiple pairs of pants and shirts and a couple of bandanas and hats. I also bought a pair of men's work boots in size ten. Brett wore size ten shoes, so that was explainable. But it was my plan to wear the shoes myself to the murder and then dump them. I hoped that no one would ever want to inventory what I'd bought at the thrift shop. But I couldn't account for every possibility. I had to take a chance somewhere, and this was one of those times.

Saturday March sixteenth was bright and sunny. I put on some of the old clothes I'd bought and painted the bathroom. It actually only took me about four hours, start to finish. The biggest part was the cleaning of the bathroom beforehand, and the taping. After I was done, I threw away the clothes I'd worn while painting. What Brett didn't see was that I still had extra clothes I'd bought and not worn. I had two flannel shirts, a blue bandanna and baseball cap, one pair of sweats, and a pair of jeans. I also had the size ten boots. I put all these things in my aerobics bag, and left the bag in the trunk of my car along with a couple of plastic garbage bags, so that I could put the clothes there afterwards. I still wasn't sure where I'd dump them, but I knew I would figure something out.

That night I went to rent a movie and stopped at the drug store. I bought some new mascara and some tanning cream, and I paid cash. Over the last several weeks I had gotten into the habit of sometimes paying cash and sometimes using my debit. I didn't want to look "sneaky" when I paid cash. But I also didn't want that list of what I'd bought easy to find.

Monday, March eighteenth dawned rainy and cold. I tried not to view that as an omen. I was already tired by the end of work, and I knew I still had aerobics and a possible murder on my plate. I was just nervous enough that I felt energized after my light dinner. I told Brett that I would go to the store after aerobics. I complained that I had a busy week and still needed to get something for Kara's class basket. Brett, sweet as usual, asked if I wanted him to go to the store. I told him no, since I'd be out anyway. I kissed him and told him I loved him. I kissed Kara and held her tight. I didn't allow myself to think about never seeing them again after I was caught at the scene and taken into police custody. I had taken the gun out on Sunday morning while Brett and Kara were both sleeping, and it was safely locked away in my gym bag in the trunk of my car.

I went in the bathroom right before I left. I tried to think of anything I'd forgotten. I was leaving my cell phone at home and pretending I'd forgotten it, because I knew that the police could check a person's location based on the cell phone records. Ironically, I had learned this from Sergeant Walter. When they were searching for a way to tie Mortenson to Mia's murder he had explained that they hoped to catch him through his cell phone records, but that unfortunately Mortenson didn't have a cell phone. I had no idea that the police could use cell phones to track a person prior to that, but I'd remembered that information when I first started planning Mortenson's death. I put my cell phone on the bedroom dresser and looked around. I was as ready as I was going to be...

I had the clothes I planned on changing into inside my gym bag. I had already decided to change at an empty construction site I had noticed about a mile from Mortenson's apartment. I just had to make sure that no one saw me. I decided at the last minute to alter my license plate again. When I went out to the garage to leave, I grabbed the roll of duct tape and put it in my gym bag too.

My stomach was a jumble of nerves, but the aerobics class helped. I sweated out a lot of my anxiety. Then I walked the track, but only half the distance I usually did, and sat in the sauna for only five minutes. I showered quickly and went out the back as usual. I was in my car and driving towards Belmont by eight thirty-five p.m.

I sped a bit and made good time to the construction site. Luckily, no one was around. The area inside the fence was actually pretty well lit up, but there was a dark area off to the side. I changed and took out the tanning cream, which I had bought in as dark a shade as possible, and covered my face and upper neck with it. Then I wound my hair up as tight as possible under a blue bandana. I covered most of my forehead with the bandana, and then put the baseball cap on top of it. I then covered my regular clothes with the two flannel shirts, the sweats, and the bulky men's jeans. I put on the size ten shoes. They felt awkward, but I wore a women's eight-and-a-half shoe, so it wasn't that bad. The last thing I put on was a pair of sterile gloves I had taken from work. Then, I took out a small lighted makeup mirror I usually kept in my bag and checked my reflection. I looked different, all right. I had been trying to look like an olive-skinned man, but I didn't know if I'd succeeded.

I walked over to where I'd parked my car in the shadows. I bent down and quickly altered the license plate in the same way I'd done on my quest to get the gun. My stint as a fake prostitute seemed long ago now. I wondered if John had reported his gun stolen. I couldn't help myself and felt a nervous giggle escape from my throat at the thought of John and his invisible penis. I mentally chastised myself and told myself to focus. I couldn't waste time thinking about that now. It was already after nine o'clock.

I drove by Mortenson's place, and saw his parking

spot was empty. I was hoping to get this over with tonight, and I didn't want to go through this again on Wednesday. My heart was pounding hard and I was sweating all over. I actually felt like I was going to throw up. I fought the nausea and kept going. I started driving towards Rainy's grocery store, and was almost there, when I saw Mortenson's car pass me. I couldn't believe it! He was about seven or eight blocks from his apartment. I wanted to turn around, but didn't want to draw any attention to myself. I waited a moment, then did a U-turn. I drove as fast as I dared. Luck was with me, and I caught up with Mortenson at the four-way stop that was two blocks from his house. I felt it was now or never. The gun was lying on the passenger seat under my gym bag, within easy reach. Mortenson had stopped at the four-way-stop, like the law-abiding citizen he pretended to be. I didn't see any other cars. For a split second I thought of just shooting him from my car, but I wasn't confident that I would hit him, or if I hit him, that the wound would kill him. I accelerated quickly and passed Mortenson's car on the left, running the four-way-stop like a crazy person. It fit my mood. I felt a little crazy. Mortenson laid on the horn, but didn't race to catch me.

I drove like a maniac to Mortenson's apartment building. I pulled around to the side of the building, far enough that my car was hidden from the parking lot. I grabbed the gun and I jumped out. I expected my legs to be rubbery, but they felt strong as I sprinted to the side of the building. I held the gun tight to my side and slightly behind my back. I knew Mortenson had to be just seconds from arriving home. I stood there and as he pulled up I started to walk slowly along the pathway. Unit number one was at the start of the path and number eight was almost to the end – there were ten units on the street level. I saw that most of the cars were in their assigned places. I knew that meant lots of potential witnesses were at home, but I couldn't turn back now.

Mortenson got out of his car and walked toward the back of his car. I realized he had been drinking. His steps were slow and thoughtful, but he was failing in his attempt to walk straight. He didn't appear to notice me. I didn't want to walk all the way over to his apartment. It was just that much farther away from my car. I realized my good luck when Mortenson stopped to open his trunk. I waited as he fumbled with his keys. He opened the trunk and bent over to look in it. I jogged over to the rear driver's side of his car, so that I was just to his left. Time seemed to slow. Mortenson was still bent down. He had a twelve pack of beer in his left hand, and a carton of eggs in his right. He saw me then, and raised his head slowly. His watery eyes showed annoyance, not anger. I realized my relief, and for the first time, I realized I was afraid of Mortenson. Although it seemed a no-brainer, I hadn't been honest with myself about that fear until just that moment. In my fantasies I had never been afraid to confront him, but I had been fooling myself. I took a step back, but straightened, determined to be brave. Mortenson put the eggs down, but didn't bother to release his grip on his beer. I held the gun behind my back in my right hand, but his eyes didn't stray from my face. "What the fuck!" he slurred.

"Gary," I said.

His slack face looked at me questioningly. "Do I know you, asshole?" he asked. When I didn't answer, he became surlier. "I SAID, do I know you, ASSWIPE? Speak the fuck up!" He dropped the beer and squared himself towards me. I saw his fists clench and knew he was ready to fight.

I had fantasized about this moment many times. In my fantasies, I opened up a barrage of gunfire on Mortenson, filling him with lead from his head to his toes. In my fantasies, I screamed, "Die, Motherfucker!" with a Rambo-like yell.

This was no fantasy, although the moment seemed surreal. I took a deep breath and forced myself to realize that this was the moment. Now or never. Do or die. (My brain whispered to me that I always thought in clichés in times of stress.) Suddenly, I found that I was no longer nervous or afraid. Maybe it was real craziness setting in, or maybe I was in the zone, the way that athletes are at their moment of truth. But I suddenly felt steady. All my hate for Mortenson filled me, a feeling stronger and deeper than rage – a feeling that surpassed uncontrolled anger. It was like a black, oily, heavy sadness that filled me up and left no room for compassion or mercy. I answered his question, calmly and quietly.

"No, Gary. You don't know me." It felt right to call

him Gary now. A three second pause ensued as I noticed that my heart was beating hard and fast again. I breathed deep and swallowed hard. "But you knew my sister." I had assumed that this moment would be one of understanding for Mortenson, and that he would comprehend that he was facing his victim's sibling. I searched his drunken face for a reaction, but he just looked at me with a smirk. Maybe he was just too drunk to fully process what I said. At any rate, I could see from his demeanor that he had sized me up as someone weak, someone who was not to be feared.

I lifted the gun, and pointed it at his face. I had the sweet satisfaction of watching his smirk fall away. I would have liked to have savored the moment, but I knew there could be no hesitation now. I pulled the trigger and saw his eyes widen in surprise, just as the hole opened up in his forehead. Strangely, I didn't hear the shot. I was fixated on Mortenson and his reaction. He continued to stand for another second, maybe two, as I shot him twice more. I saw the second shot open a hole in his left cheek and the third hit his neck, before gravity pulled him to the pavement. He fell, and I leaned over him, shooting once more in the center of his chest. "Her name was Mia," I whispered. "Her name was Mia."

15

I ran to my car, holding the gun against my stomach. I didn't want anyone to see it in my hand. I got into my car and drove quickly away toward the back of Mortenson's building, careful not to give the neighbors out front a chance to see my car. When I was several blocks away, I stripped off the baseball cap and bandana, and the flannel shirts, shoving them into one of the garbage bags I'd left open inside my gym bag. This was tricky, as I didn't dare stop driving away from the scene, but I felt safer after changing my appearance. My shoulder length hair was now clearly visible, and I was wearing a short-sleeved workout shirt, which was clearly different than what any witnesses to the killing would have seen. I was well aware, though, that the clothes and gun were still in my car and that if the police stopped me, I was done. I was drenched in sweat, and my hands were shaking. It was hard to concentrate on my driving. I felt very strange – almost euphoric, but scared at the same time. I noticed that tears were running down my cheeks, although I didn't feel like I was crying. I didn't know if this was a normal reaction, or whether I had completely lost my mind. But I could wonder about my sanity later. I was too busy to dwell on it then.

I hadn't noticed whether Mortenson's blood had gotten on me. If so, I imagined it was only on the front of my clothes. After watching a show on forensic science, Brett mentioned that the police often found trace evidence of blood inside cars during murder investigations. With that in mind, I'd taken an old blanket from the trunk and thrown it over the driver's seat of my car after I'd changed into my disguise at the construction site. I'd also taken my gym towel and laid it over the floorboard of the driver's seat. The accelerator and brake weren't covered, but that was about it. If there was blood, I hoped it would get on the blanket and towels, not the car seat or floorboard.

I looked at the dashboard clock as I entered the freeway, and was amazed to see it was only nine twenty-seven. I heard sirens in the distance, and was relieved that they seemed so far away. I still needed to ditch the clothes and gun, but first I needed to put some distance between me and Belmont.

I made my way toward the mall. I got off the freeway two exits early, because I could see some construction equipment at a vacant lot from there. I had calmed a bit now, but my hands were still shaking. I parked in a dark area on the perimeter of the construction site and got out of the car. I bent down and took the duct tape off the license plates and put the used tape in the garbage bag, along with the clothes, the hat, the bandana, and the gun. I grabbed my tennis shoes, along with the blanket and towel off the driver's side of the car, and went into a Port-A-Potty. I dropped the blanket and gym towel onto the filthy floor of the tiny bathroom. I kept my plastic gloves on, and started dumping the items, one by one, into the stinking hole. I didn't want them secured in the garbage bag if they were found. I wanted them covered in lots and lots of other people's DNA. I was starting to feel anxious, but reminded myself to be grateful that things had gone smoothly so far. I finished by stripping off the men's boots, jeans and sweats I'd worn, leaving only my workout pants still on. I dropped the boots, clothing, blanket, and gym towel down into the abyss, and then took off the plastic gloves and threw them down as well. I had one final step. I went back to my gym bag, where I had put a wet washcloth into a zip-lock bag before leaving home. I took out the washcloth and cleaned my face and neck of the dark-shaded foundation, then threw the remaining makeup and the washcloth down into the tank. Afterwards, I stood in the Port-A-Potty for a few moments and tried to think of anything I'd forgotten. Everything I'd worn and held during the murder was gone. I wondered about my door handle and steering wheel. I didn't think there was blood on them from the gloves, but I wondered about gun-powder. Could they check for that on a steering wheel? Probably. I went to my console and found a couple of hand-wipes I kept there for Kara's face and hands. I washed off the steering wheel and the gear-shift, and then both the inside and outside of the door handles. Then, feeling a bit panicky, I opened another hand-wipe and wiped off the accelerator and brake pedal. Finally, I went to the Port-a-Potty and threw the wipes down the hole. I didn't know if I'd missed a step, but I felt I'd done everything I could to destroy the evidence tying me to Mortenson. It took longer than I thought though, and it was already nine-fifty. I quickly drove back onto the freeway and started reviewing my story as I drove.

I walked into the mall just before ten. At the last minute I decided to park where I always parked – surveillance cameras be damned. I didn't want to act suspiciously by changing the entrance I normally used, but I also just couldn't deal with walking any extra distance. Unfortunately, the adrenaline rush that had briefly spiked me with energy immediately following the killing was gone, and I felt like I could lie down on the spot and sleep for a week. I tried to walk at my regular pace throughout the length of the mall, but I felt utterly exhausted. Luckily though, just being in such a familiar place helped calm my racing thoughts. As I had driven to the mall, I had actively fought away thoughts of arrest and prison. Even as I tried to fight it down, I felt my panic building up until I was afraid that I would fall to my knees and confess at my first glimpse of an authority figure. But the mundane atmosphere of the mall – the sounds of my feet on the walkway, the chatter of the salesmen at the cell phone kiosk, the Muzak in the background – was calming. The rest of the night had been so surreal, and this was bringing me back to reality. I finally bought a yoga mat that came with a free water bottle at Youngman's. I called Brett from a payphone and told him I didn't have my cell phone. I asked if I had left it at home and he said I had. He joked that he actually started to call me and let me know, but then heard my cell phone ringing in the house. We both laughed. I apologized to Brett for running late and told him I'd decided to go shopping for Kara's school's auction basket gift tonight instead of to the grocery store, to get it over with. I complained that I had driven almost all the way to the grocery store before changing my mind and driving to the shopping center closest to our house. Then I decided that the mall would have a better selection after all, and had to drive all the way out here. I apologized for being so late and said that I would be home as soon as I could.

After we hung up, I thought some more about my timeline. I wanted this clear in my head before I got home. I knew the shopping center closest to home was about fifteen minutes from the YMCA. If I had driven almost all the way to the grocery store first, and then back towards the shopping center, I would have lost about thirty-five minutes. Then it was about a twenty-five minute drive to the mall. So that was an hour in driving time. I left the YMCA at about eight thirty-five, although I would normally have stayed there until almost nine. I wasn't wearing a watch though, and didn't think anyone could expect me to be exact on my timeline. If asked what time I'd left the YMCA, I'd say I hadn't noticed exactly, and that it was around my regular time. All that driving back and forth would have put me arriving at the mall around ten p.m., the actual time that I had arrived.

It was a good, simple story. The authorities could verify that I was at the YMCA and at the mall, and would be hard-pressed to prove I wasn't driving back and forth in between. And I figured I'd continue to run errands after aerobics class in the future, just to remain consistent. I knew there was no such thing as a perfect murder, but I felt I had done a good job in covering all the bases. All I had to do now was wait and hope I wasn't caught.

I ended up leaving the mall at quarter till eleven. I realized I was starving and drove through the drive-thru at the Dairy Barn, ordering my favorite, a Choco-Cookie Snowstorm, which was basically a chunky cookie milkshake. Afterwards, I parked in the lot so that I could enjoy the treat in private. I was celebrating. Mortenson was dead. Dead! He could never hurt anyone again. I might get caught, but there was no bringing him back to life! I took a deep breath and felt myself relax and smile – really smile. I didn't lie to myself and pretend I felt remorse for what I'd done. I was thrilled that he was dead, and I felt happy and proud that I was the one who had killed him. I mentally patted myself on the back. I had done it! I took another bite and lifted my spoon in a private toast. "To Gary Mortenson. May you rot in Hell." I felt really and truly good, and I wanted to remember this moment. I allowed myself to savor every bite of my treat before starting on the road home.

I got home and Brett was asleep in bed. He half-woke up as I crawled between the sheets and pulled me towards him, even as he fell back asleep. That was just what I needed. I snuggled in close, with my back to him, and felt my body relax. I hadn't realized that I was so tensed up. Once I relaxed, though, I started to crumble. I still felt a sense of accomplishment, but too much had happened in too short a time for me to hold it all in. Realizing that I wasn't as tough as I'd hoped, I gave into the tears. I don't know if they were tears of sadness, fear, or relief, but I let them flow, and cried myself to sleep.

The next morning I felt pretty much back to normal. In the bathroom I looked at myself in the mirror. I had a strange thought that I looked the same this morning as I had yesterday morning. It was amazing to me that killing someone hadn't changed the way I looked. Time to get on with my life, I thought. I did what I wanted to do, and I can move on now. The power of positive thinking.

I got up and got Kara to school, and went to work. I didn't want to change my routine at all, and I didn't usually listen to the news in the morning. But I was curious whether Mortenson's death had made the news. I assumed that Sergeant Walter would call me or stop by sometime in the next couple days to tell me that Mortenson was dead. I didn't want to think about that conversation too much, because I wanted to keep my reaction to the news as spontaneous as possible. I made a mental note though to ask how Mortenson died. I certainly couldn't make the mistake of assuming that he'd been murdered, rather than having died of a drug overdose or in a car accident, or of a heart attack. Sergeant Walter wasn't stupid, and I couldn't be, either. At least I wouldn't have to fake being happy he was dead. Sergeant Walter would understand that. I was willing to bet that Sergeant Walter would be pretty thrilled when he got the news himself. And since Mortenson's murder didn't happen in our town, he wouldn't be investigating it. I hoped that in itself would distance any focus on me or my family.

So I was truly not pretending any surprise when I arrived at work to a barrage of news crews. As I got out of my car, they swarmed me from all sides. "How do you feel knowing that your sister's murderer was murdered himself?"

"What were you doing when you first heard that Gary Mortenson had been killed?"

"Have the police questioned you regarding the murder of Gary Mortenson?"

That last question did scare me, but I was so overwhelmed by the cameras and microphones surrounding me, that I just stood there like a deer in the headlights. I knew I had to look shocked and surprised, because that was how I felt. How did the media get here so fast? Do they sleep with a police scanner in their ears? What a bunch of vultures! At any rate, I tried to answer their questions as I walked, and got in a few questions of my own. "Did you say that Gary Mortenson was murdered? Are you sure? When?" When asked where I was when I first heard about it, I answered, "This is the first I've heard about it." I finally managed to get to the office door, and went inside. For a moment I just stood there, overwhelmed. I told my coworkers I wanted to be alone to collect my thoughts and my boss offered me his office. I went in and called Brett.

"Brett, Gary Mortenson is dead."

"What?" he gasped. "Where are you? Are you okay?"

I sighed. "I'm at work. I found out when I got here. The media's here. I don't know if I can stay at work today. It might be too disruptive."

"Kate, can you drive home? Do you want me to come get you?"

"No, I'm okay. I need to talk to my boss and see if it's all right for me to take the day off. I want to talk to Sergeant Walter, but I don't want to call him from here."

Brett sounded a little excited about this news himself. I wasn't surprised when he offered to make the call to the Sergeant.

"I'll call him, honey. You just get home. I have a meeting this morning that I can't miss, but I'll be home around twelve-thirty. Will you be okay until then?"

"Sure, Brett, I'll be fine. Oh My God! What about Mom? I've got to call her." I didn't have to fake my alarm. I didn't want my mom hearing about this from the media.

Suddenly, I decided what to do next.

"Brett, I'm going to go to Mom's when I leave here. I'll either be there, or at home, depending on how she does with the news. I might need to stay with her."

"Sure, honey, that sounds good. I'll call you before I leave work."

I went and talked to my boss. He told me to go ahead and leave, and to take tomorrow off if I needed to. I thanked him for being so understanding, and really meant it. I didn't want to leave immediately, because two of the news crews were still outside. So I sat in the break room and drank a cup of coffee. The vultures were gone within about twenty more minutes, and I drove to my mom's.

When I pulled up I could see Mom vacuuming through the window. Rather than reassuring me, it made me wonder if she'd already heard the news. I remembered that she cleaned her house from top to bottom when Mia died, in expectation of the company she must have known would come – and come they did, for a whole week after Mia died and up to the day of her funeral. If Mom had heard the news about Mortenson, she was probably cleaning just in case anyone stopped by to talk about it.

I stopped on the porch for a moment. I hoped Mom took this news okay. If it hit her hard, I would be the only one to blame. That thought scared me.

I knocked, but she didn't hear me because of the vacuum. I rang the doorbell, and still no answer. I walked over to the flower bed and stood in front of the window and waved my arms as if I was signaling a rescue plane.

She caught sight of the movement from the corner of her eye and smiled and waved back to me. She turned off the vacuum and had the door open before I got back to the porch.

"Hi honey! What a nice surprise!" Then, realizing it was a work day, she paled a bit. "Is everything okay? Kara and Brett are okay?"

"They're great, Mom. But I have some news. I'm not sure if it's good or bad news, but I wanted to be the one to tell you."

Mom motioned to Dad's chair. I always sat in it when I came. Mom sat down in her slider-rocker. She seemed relaxed, now that she knew that Brett and Kara were all right.

"What's your news?"

"Apparently someone killed Gary Mortenson. The reporters were at my work this morning and I had to leave. I wasn't sure if you'd heard. I'm surprised the reporters weren't here, too."

"Well, honey, I went to the grocery store early this morning. Could be they came by and I wasn't home."

I was a little surprised. Mom didn't seem fazed by the news. I also couldn't really read her reaction. She didn't seem particularly happy or sad, just kind of matter-of-fact.

"Mom, did you hear about it before I came? You don't seem surprised."

"No, you're the first to tell me. But I'm not surprised. An animal like that was sure to be put down eventually. And God forgive me, I won't pretend that I'm sad about it!"

I smiled at her. "You and me both. I didn't hear who killed him, or how. Brett said he was going to call Sergeant Walter for some details. I was worried that either the reporters would upset you, or the news itself would upset you. I was always hoping they would get some proof and send him to prison."

Mom smiled. "Well, of course it would have been wonderful for him to have gone to prison. But then I would always wonder about him getting out. At least this way, we don't have to worry about him any more – for Kara's sake and all those other girls out there. And it's a kind of Karma, isn't it?"

I laughed, because I had never known my mother to talk about Karma in the past. "It's Karma, all right!"

Mom offered to make me some coffee or tea, and I chose Chamomile Tea. She took out some shortbread cookies she had, and we sat and talked about all the things that mattered, Kara and Brett, yard work, the sales at the mall, and how Robert and his family were doing. This is what matters, I thought. Family, just family.

I stayed at Mom's until one and then went home. As I walked out onto the porch, Mom said something that made my heart sink as though affixed to a leaden weight.

"Kate, remember you said that Mortenson's mother was in court that day? Let's keep her in our prayers. God help that poor woman. No one deserves the hell of losing her child, especially to murder. So let's pray for her, Kate." Mom blinked back a tear, and I knew she was remembering Mia. I nodded my agreement to pray for my victim's mother, and felt the light, quick pinpricks of guilt and shame poke at my consciousness. With that, Mom gave me a quick hug and told me to drive carefully. As I walked to my car, I did my best to shake off any negativity. No one said this would be easy.

When I got home I found a message on my answering machine from Sergeant Walter. He said he'd he had tried to reach me at work, and that my boss told him I was aware of the news. He left his number and asked me to call if I had questions.

I decided not to call him until after I had talked to Brett. If Brett talked to him and got the details, I wouldn't have to call at all.

Brett got home at one-fifteen and apologized profusely for the delay. He said that his meeting ran long and that he called my mom's and she said that I had just left. He hoped to beat me home, but there was a traffic backup from an earlier accident that slowed him. I reassured him that I was fine and that he needn't have rushed.

I asked him if he had called Sergeant Walter, and he said he hadn't had a chance before his meeting. "I'll call him now, okay? Then we can go get Kara from school," he said.

I sat in the living room and listened to Brett on the phone. I couldn't tell much from the conversation. I was anxious for Brett's update.

Brett turned to me after he hung up. "Well, I guess

Gary Mortenson was still living over in Belmont. His neighbors called after they heard shots. They saw a man running away from the back of Mortenson's car. When someone looked out, they saw Mortenson laying there. He'd been shot. They haven't caught the guy, but the Sergeant said they're just at the beginning of the investigation. Sergeant Walter said that it could be anything at this point, from an angry co-worker, to a drug deal gone bad. To be honest, he didn't sound too torn up that Mortenson is dead."

Brett engulfed me in a hug. "Are you all right?"

"Yeah. It's kind of weird. I guess I feel happy he's dead, but he was still never held responsible for killing Mia. It still feels like he got away with it. But Mom and I are both in agreement that the world's better off without Mortenson."

"That makes three of us!"

After that, Brett and I went and got Kara from school and had a nice dinner. We watched the news, and Mortenson's murder was the lead story. From the news account, it sounded like robbery was thought to be a possible motive, as Mortenson's wallet was gone. Huh, I thought. I should have taken his wallet. I wondered who did, or if he had just left it somewhere in his drunken state. Or maybe one of the witnesses who called police decided to relieve him of his possessions prior to police arrival. At any rate, the robbery theory was good news for me.

I called Lisa that night after Kara was tucked in.

Even though we didn't see each other much, Lisa continued to be my best girlfriend and surrogate sister. Lisa always put a positive spin on things, and I anticipated an upbeat conversation with her. I needed that, as I was still feeling a little funny about what Mortenson's mom must be going through.

Lisa didn't disappoint. "That is fucking wonderful news!" she yelled into the phone after I dropped the bombshell. "Did he suffer? God, I hope he suffered! Did they let you see his body? Who did it? I want to nominate them for an award!" I started giggling. I'm not a giggler, except around Lisa. She does it every time. I knew better than to try and answer while Lisa was wound up. I would answer when she stopped to take a breath. "Let's throw a party. A huge, Ding Dong the Fucker's Dead party! Let's have it at my place! My treat!" Still no sign of stopping or breathing. "This is fucking FABULOUS! I mean, FABULOUS! I'm so HAPPY I'm almost ORGASMIC!" Ahh, a pause. I was still chuckling over the orgasm reference as I finally spoke up.

"Lisa, I don't think a party is appropriate under the circumstances. I mean, he might have some family who are grieving." Saying this aloud did bring me down a bit, but Lisa's excitement was contagious, and it pushed any feelings of guilt to the side.

"To answer your question, the police don't know who did it. They think it might have been a robbery."

"Good. I hope he was scared shitless! I hope he begged for his life like a little girl!" Suddenly, Lisa sobered. "I'm sorry honey. That was a bad choice of words. You know what I mean."

I wasn't fazed. I had learned long ago that I needed to listen to what Lisa meant, not what she said. She had never been diplomatic, but always had a heart of gold.

"I know, Lisa. Don't worry about it."

She brightened. "Okay, so no party. But I INSIST on taking you and Kara shopping. At least three new outfits, each! My treat!"

"Lisa, Kara still hasn't worn all the clothes you bought her during your last visit. If you insist, you can take us out to lunch or dinner, and buy Kara a small gift. I appreciate it, but if you keep going through money this way, you'll be in the poorhouse."

Lisa did her best foreign movie star imitation. "Dahling, I have millions and millions! I vill never be in za poorhaus!" I laughed. Lisa was right, of course. She wasn't frivolous with her money, only generous. She gave a lot to charity, and spent money on friends and family, but not much on herself. She came across as an airhead sometimes, but she was a pretty savvy business-woman. She knew how much money she had, and she wouldn't squander it. The truth was, Lisa never cared anything about money anyway. She was fairly fashion-obsessed when she was younger, but now her main obsession was children. She wanted desperately to be a mother, but felt strongly she wanted to raise her child with the love of her life. Alas, he was still unidentified.

"Okay, a spa day and a dinner for you, and a gift for Kara.

And a new golf club for Brett! But that's my final offer!"

The rest of the week went well. I took the next day off of work, just because my boss had encouraged it. I continued with my aerobics classes and running errands afterwards. I actually enjoyed going to the grocery store when it was quiet, although I would have preferred to do it when I wasn't exhausted from a workout. But aerobics would be over with soon.

I was surprised then, when I got home from work on Thursday night and saw Sergeant Walter sitting out front in his car. He got out as soon as I pulled into the driveway. I was scared – no, terrified. Strangely, only one word ran through my mind. Karma. I knew something horrible had happened.

Sergeant Walter walked up to me looking very sober. I felt my legs go weak. I started to see spots in front of my eyes. "Is it Brett or Kara?" I was barely able to strangle out the words, as the sobs came. Sergeant Walter grabbed my elbow, as I started to sink to the ground. "Oh, Kate, no! Brett and Kara are fine! That's not why I'm here! I just need to talk to you. Your family's fine!" He was smiling and looking at me with reassurance, and with pity. I could see he was telling me the truth. I felt my legs get stronger and I was able to stand up straight, but I was shaking uncontrollably. Sergeant Walter asked for my keys, and he unlocked the door and walked me inside. All the way, he kept reassuring me that everything was fine. I think he was as shocked as I was by my reaction to seeing him at my home.

I don't know why I reacted that way, but whatever it was had hit me like a ton of bricks. I guess maybe I was fearful of ramifications for killing Mortenson, after all. Because my thought hadn't been that the sergeant was there to question me about the murder. My thought had been a certainty that God had punished me by taking my family away. Sergeant Walter deposited me on the couch and went to get me a glass of water. He came back in and watched me while I drank it.

"Are you feeling better, Kate? I'm sorry I startled you. I should have called ahead. It's just that I just got some news about Mortenson, and I didn't want you to hear it from the media, like you did before. I felt just terrible about that, but I was working an urgent case, and I had worked all night on the night he was killed. I had gone home about four in the morning and slept 'til ten, and then went back into work. So by the time I heard the news, the media was already bothering you."

"No, it's fine, Sergeant. I don't know why I reacted that way. I just assumed it was bad news. I'm fine now. What did you want to tell me?"

"Well, I think you'll feel like this is good news. After Mortenson's murder, the Belmont Sheriff's Office searched Gary Mortenson's apartment, as well as his work locker and a storage locker he had. They found a box full of surveillance type pictures of a woman in her early twenties, along with a calendar with April twenty-third circled." He paused and saw by the look on my face that I understood. The same day he murdered Mia.

"That's right. The same day Mia was killed, but this year. Anyway, I can't share all of the information with you, but suffice it to say, there are indications that he was stalking this girl."

I started to shake again. "The girl? Is she all right?"

"I'm sorry, Kate. I'm really bungling this. I didn't mean to scare you. She's fine. Luckily, a few of the pictures showed the place she worked in the background. It was this supermarket called Rainy's. The Belmont Sheriff's Office was able to identify her. It turns out the girl is a checker there. She remembers Mortenson coming in almost every night. He would usually only buy beer, and he would always go through her line. He was always chatting her up, and she was polite, but not encouraging. She said that she thought he was creepy."

Feeling dimwitted, I asked, "So she's all right. I mean, he never did anything to her?"

"Right. But he had so many pictures of her, and not just at her work. He had pictures of her leaving her apartment and arriving home. He was definitely stalking her. He had written her name on the date of April twenty-third on his calendar, and circled it. Now that he's dead, we'll never know for sure, but it seems pretty clear that he had plans to hurt her."

Sergeant Walter paused and smiled gently. "Brett said that you and he were happy that Mortenson was dead, but felt that he had still gotten away with Mia's murder. That's true, of course. But I thought it might help to know that he was killed before he victimized another young woman. I can't say that I'm happy he was murdered, but I'm very glad that this young lady is safe."

"Well, Sergeant, you're a better person than I am, because I'm very happy he's dead. I was always worried in the back of my mind that he might hurt someone else, or even come for me or Kara. I feel so much safer now. But you're right. I'm sure he has some family who are grieving now. Murder can't ever be a good thing." I paused, because I really believed that Mortenson's murder was a good thing and I felt like a hypocrite for saying it wasn't. I may have imagined it, but I think that Sergeant Walter understood what I was thinking and agreed with me. I went on. "So much violence in the world. I don't know how you do your job."

"Oh, it's pretty satisfying, at times." He paused, having said what he came to say. "Well, Kate, I just wanted to deliver the news in person. I'm sure the media is going to get the information. The girl in question was approached at her job today, and I was afraid that you and your family would be next. But I'm sorry I gave you a scare."

"No, that's not your fault. I'm just jumpy. This was good news. I'm glad the other woman is safe. I wouldn't want any other family to go through what we've been through."

"Absolutely. Well, unless you have any questions, I'll be going now."

"No, I'll walk you out. Thanks again for coming out. I'm sure you have other things to do."

We walked out to the car. "Spring's just about here.

Feels good to see the sun a little bit. Your garden's nice."

I looked down and saw a couple crocuses were popping up. They hadn't been there even two days before. It was nice to see a sign of spring.

"Thanks, Sergeant. And I wanted to thank you for everything you've done for our family. I guess now that Mortenson is dead, we won't be hearing from you again."

"I guess not. But it was a pleasure meeting you and your family. It's hard to put this delicately, but a lot of times the people I deal with are living a pretty high-risk lifestyle. It's not like they deserve the bad things that happen to them, but some of the crimes most likely wouldn't occur if they had conducted themselves more responsibly and stayed away from drugs and running the streets. So when I meet a family as nice and responsible as yours, it's a double edged sword. It's nice to deal with good people, but it seems even more tragic when they are victimized. I'll be honest. We investigated Mia's lifestyle and basically kind of tore her life apart, trying to find a tie to Mortenson. She was just a sweet, hard-working girl. Everyone we spoke with had nothing but good things to say about her. So maybe I lied a bit when I said I was never happy about a murder. I am pretty damn happy that Mortenson's dead. But that's off the record."

"Absolutely, Sergeant, your secret's safe with me." We smiled at one another, and I stuck out my hand for a goodbye handshake.

Then, impulsively, I hugged him and he gave a little

squeeze back. He was such a good man. I hoped that he stayed safe and happy. I knew he had a wife and son to go home to.

I went back inside. My emotions were all jumbled up. I had been absolutely sure that something horrible had happened to Brett or Kara, and equally sure that it was a punishment from God for what I'd done. And then I got this good news instead. I realized that I had been awaiting my penance from God for killing Mortenson. I felt all tangled up inside, like I'd dodged a bullet. But would a penance still come to me? I decided to ignore my fears for now, and start dinner. Brett and Kara would be home any minute.

That night, the investigation into Mortenson's murder was the top story on the six o'clock news. Brett was helping Kara with her math homework, but I was eager to watch the story. It was soon apparent that there wasn't much to report about his murder, and the story remained focused on what police had learned about Mortenson's life during their investigation. I already had the bulk of the information about the girl at the supermarket from Sergeant Walter, so I was prepared for that.

What did shock me was the unexpected interview with Mortenson's mother, Candace. She'd been preparing for his funeral, which was scheduled for Saturday. A female reporter had interviewed Candace Mortenson at home. If the reporter hadn't identified her, I wouldn't have recognized this haggard woman as the same one I'd seen in the courtroom at Mortenson's arraignment.

I hoped it might have been her cancer that had altered her appearance to this gaunt caricature of the woman I'd seen, but I knew better. I'd seen a similar change in my own mirror following Mia's death. I recognized the ravages of grief when I saw it now. Candace was speaking now and I unconsciously leaned in closer to the television.

"I know that people think my boy is some kind of a monster. But I'm his mother. I know him. He's a good boy." She seemed to realize she'd mistakenly referred to her son in the present tense. She faltered and choked on her tears, as the reporter pulled away and started to end the segment. Suddenly the old woman's weathered hand grabbed onto the reporter's bicep with what looked like surprising strength. She wasn't finished. "He was an altar boy growing up, did you know that? And he took care of me." After a pause, she continued. "He had a horrible time in school. You know, children can be so cruel. Gary was always very shy. But those kids, they teased him mercilessly. Called him names. Made going to school like torture for him. It got so bad, but no one at the school even tried to help. Gary ended up trying to kill himself while he was in high school. Anyone would have, after what he'd been through. Even then, no one tried to help. No one understood. They just thought he was more of a freak." The reporter looked truly uncomfortable now, and her time limit for this interview had probably been exceeded. But Candace was on a roll.

"But you know what my baby did? He pulled himself up. Without a single friend to help him, he decided to live. And later on he went back to that high school and spoke at an assembly on bullying. I was so proud of him! He told me that several different students came up to him and said he'd changed their lives. They told him they would never forget him."

The camera panned in closely now, and I was shocked to see the mother's pride still evident on the old woman's face. The echoes of pride faded as her expression changed to one of determination. She spoke strongly. "Anyone can make a mistake. My boy wasn't all good. But he wasn't all bad either. Who knows what good he might have done, if he'd lived? He was working hard. He just needed a chance. He wasn't a monster. He WASN'T! He was a good boy." She trailed off as the tears rolled down her cheeks. Softly she whispered, "He was my baby."

"Thank you, Ms. Mortenson. We're very sorry for your loss. This is Amanda Whitaker reporting, for Channel Seven News."

I sat back, feeling slightly sickened. I had done this. I'd done the same thing to this nice old woman that Mortenson had done to us. I'd ripped a mother's child from her forever.

I sat there for a few minutes, mulling it all over. I remembered Mia's story about the man who spoke at the assembly on bullying. Was that Mortenson? I had to concede that it was possible, but didn't think it likely. Surely the police would have mentioned it, had Mortenson attended the same high school as Mia. No, I didn't think he had. The town was small, and someone would have mentioned it.

I sat there for a long time, thinking.

Maybe it was a rationalization, but I ended up concluding that a parent's love is the very definition of unconditional love. I was truly sorry that Mortenson's mother was going through this pain. But Mortenson had to die. I still felt I'd made the right decision. Mortenson could have spent his life living with monks and helping the poor, and it still wouldn't make up for what he did to my sister.

I could accept that what I did was wrong. I murdered a man, I could admit that now. But it was the lesser of two evils. Letting Mortenson live would have been worse. I felt sure he would have killed again. Someone has to be willing to make the tough choices, I thought. This time, it had been me. Yes, I thought. Mortenson died in the nick of time.

That night, I dreamed of Mia for the first time in a long while. It was a conversation we had around Valentine's Day the year she died. She'd just gotten paid and had invited me out to lunch at La Pinta's, a hole-in-the-wall Mexican food café.

At the start of the dream, I laughed to myself and wondered if I'd gone to bed hungry, as I saw the memory of myself delving into the chips and salsa.

"Why are men so weird?" Mia was asking. "I mean, yesterday I was at the mall, and I stopped to look at Valentine cards. I was looking at cards for Mom, and there was this guy doing the same thing. I thought it was kind of sweet, and I smiled at him. Smiled, Kate! Smiled. Didn't say I wanted to have sex with him. Didn't ask him out. Nothing. Smiled!"

I had been following along as I chewed my chips. I knew she had to have a point.

"Okay, I'll bite," I intentionally punned as I crunched loudly into another chip. "Pray tell, what happened at the card store to get you in such a tizzy?"

"Well..." Mia paused as she wiped an errant drop of salsa from her chin. "Right after I smiled at him, this guy takes the card in his hand and runs it across his crotch, and then just kind of holds it there. Then he asks, like he's being serious, 'How do you like my selection?' and looks down at his crotch. Can you believe that? What a creep!"

I laughed. "Gross. What'd you do?"

Mia laughed too. "Well, normally I probably would have just walked away. But I was really pissed. That's something you expect some loser to say in a bar, not at a Hallmark store, for God's sake! So I said, I think you definitely need to find a MUCH BIGGER selection! Then I walked away."

"That's my girl. That put him in his place."

Mia sobered a bit. "Well, that's what I thought, but he looked really disappointed, like he actually thought I'd bite at his clever line. And then after that he just glared at me, like he was really mad. He didn't seem to be the least bit embarrassed. So all it did was ruin my chance to get a card at that store."

"It's like I told you, baby sister," I said. "Boys are stupid!"

I woke up wondering if I'd dreamt of that conversation for a reason. I figured it was all that talk from Mortenson's mom about bullying and social outcasts. I didn't know, and I reminded myself that it didn't really matter. The man was rude to Mia, and Mia said something that he may have found offensive in return. We all have thousands of random encounters with strangers throughout our lives, and I'm sure we've all been rude to a stranger on occasion, even accidentally. It didn't mean we deserved to die. Had that man been Morteson? I would never know.

I knew I was still looking for the answer to the mystery of "Why Mia?" It was hard for me to admit that I would never know how or why Mortenson chose my sister, or whether he had stalked her beforehand. I told myself that these things weren't important, and that I should stop worrying about it. Killing Mortenson was supposed to make this all go away, I thought. I was supposed to be at peace now.

During the following weeks, though, I was a bit disconcerted to realize that I was still spending a fair amount of time thinking about Mortenson. I was thinking about Mia's murder a lot too. I'd thought that killing Mortenson would be the final healing piece of the puzzle for me, and that I'd never have to think about any of this again, but I was wrong. It was all still on my mind.

And what I questioned most of all was my reaction to what I'd done, and why I'd done it in the first place.

I found that I had an utter lack of remorse for killing Mortenson, which I would have thought would be a good thing. But it worried me now. I wondered if whatever it was that predisposed Mortenson to kill was also present in me. Candace Mortenson's interview had gotten to me. She'd said that no one was all good, and no one was all bad. I'd known that of course, but hearing her say it while she was remembering her baby, who'd grown up to be a killer, made it more real for me.

Motivation aside, I had successfully and cold-heartedly planned and carried out a murder. I seemed to be good at it, as I didn't regret my actions, and hadn't yet been caught. Did this make me defective in some way - more bad than good - or was the ability to murder just an aptitude I'd stumbled upon? Maybe I was like the English teacher who goes to war, and comes back with a stack of medals. Maybe I just had whatever it is that makes some people good at killing when it's necessary to kill.

I wondered about Heaven and Hell, and wished sometimes that I didn't believe in God. According to my faith, I would be forgiven if I truly repented, but it didn't look like that was likely to happen. I was too glad that Mortenson was dead.

I gave all of this a lot of thought, and in the end, this was my conclusion.

I didn't feel guilty for killing Mortenson, but I felt pretty damned guilty for not feeling guilty about it.

Life went on, of course, and time flew. Work was fine

and everyone was healthy. Mom seemed to blossom with age, and in fact got a gentleman friend who took her to dinner and dancing every Saturday night. Lisa and Kara and I started a tradition of a twice-yearly spa-day together. Brett continued to love cop shows and golf.

When Kara was eight and a half, I learned I was pregnant. Brett and I were thrilled. Brett claimed not to care whether the baby was a girl or boy, but I knew he wanted a boy to round out our family. The penance I'd feared had never come. Life was good.

Lisa had met a computer genius or "geek" as she lovingly called him, who was about five years her senior. He had plenty of his own money from a computer program he had developed, and it was obvious that he adored Lisa. They had married in June of last year, and I had never seen Lisa so happy. She loved her first husband, but he was so much older than she was, and this was just different. "Computer geek" Mitchell was actually not a computer geek, just a genius. He was an avid snow-boarder and skier, and enjoyed boating and rock-climbing as well. They were always flying off for adventures, and I was thrilled for my friend.

When I was four months pregnant, Lisa called.

"Hello?" I said as I answered the phone.

"Kate..." Nothing but sobbing. My stomach dropped. What had happened? "Please, God!" I thought, although I didn't yet know what I was asking for, other than for everything to be all right. "Lisa, take a breath, honey. Tell me what's wrong."

More hiccupping sobs were my only answer. "Kate. Kate." She was trying to talk, but couldn't get the words out between her sobs. Just as I started to really panic, she finally was able to tell me. "Katie. I'm pregnant!"

Lisa's daughter was born when our son Michael was three months old. Lisa asked me if I would mind if she named her daughter Mia. Through laughter and tears, I gave my blessing.

**One** weekend morning when Kara was almost ten, she and I went over to take Mom out to breakfast. It was fun for us to occasionally have a "girl-party" as Kara called it. Mom wasn't quite ready to go when we arrived, so I helped myself to a cup of coffee and sat down at the kitchen table. "Sorry to keep you waiting! I was trying to clean out that back closet this morning and time just got away from me."

"No problem," I replied as I sipped my coffee. "What's in the back closet?"

"Oh, this and that. You know what a pack-rat I am. But this morning I actually had a plan." With that, Mom emerged from the bathroom. "I have something here for you, Kate."

I looked up, although I wasn't surprised. Mom usually asked me if I wanted something before she threw it out. I was surprised, though, when I saw her carrying an old shoe box. "What's that?"

Mom went and got her coffee cup. "If you're not in

175

too big a hurry, do you mind if I have another half a cup before we go?"

"Sure, no hurry," I answered.

I wondered why Mom was acting a little strangely. She normally would have either handed me the box, or told me what was in it. Now, though, she filled her coffee, and sat down, placing the box to her right.

"Remember when your Dad died, and we weren't sure where he had put the will for a few days? It gave us a bit of a scare."

"I remember," I said, not sure where Mom was going with this. Maybe she was going to give me a copy of her will.

She explained. "Well, one night not too long after that Mia moved back home, and we had stayed up late talking about different things. I mentioned to her that when she got a bit older that she should be sure and make a will. I remember she laughed, and asked who she could leave her student loan debts to! Anyway, somehow we started talking about valuables, and jewelry, and she brought up that fairy necklace she used to be so crazy about when she was a little girl."

I gasped. "Tinkerbelle?"

"Yes, that's the one. Well, anyway, back then she said that she was going to give it to her daughter if she ever had one. But since we were originally talking about wills, she actually mentioned that if she died before she had a daughter, that she'd like you to have it for Kara."

"What!" I was stunned. I couldn't believe I hadn't heard any of this before. Tears sprang into my eyes in an instant.

"See honey, I thought it might make you emotional. That's one of the reasons I've been a little late in giving it to you. To be honest, those first few years I just forgot completely about that conversation with Mia. I had packed away all her jewelry. For some reason, maybe because Kara's getting older, I just happened to think about it the other day. And I thought I'd better go and find it." Mom smiled and pushed the box over to me. "So it's yours now."

I opened the box and saw a glimpse of cheap chain peeking out from inside a paper towel with a motif I recognized from my childhood. I carefully unwrapped the necklace and took it from the box. Tinkerbelle looked exactly as I remembered. In my memory I could still see Mia kissing the necklace good night at bedtime. I caressed it with my fingers for a few moments, then laid it back inside the box. "Kara," I called. "I have something very special for you from your Aunt Mia."

Mom squeezed my hand as Kara ran in from the living room. She squealed with delight when she saw the necklace. "Wow! Can I wear it to breakfast?"

A few days later, I had a dream about Mia's eighth grade dance. Mia had been getting ready and I had gone over to see her outfit. This was actually not her first real dance, as the school had started giving them in the seventh grade by then. Another key difference between Mia's eighth grade dance and mine was that Mia seemed not the least bit nervous while she got ready.

"Wow, Mia, you look really beautiful," I told her,

because she did. "I know!" She laughed. It had been a joke between us that she always said, "I know" when I gave her a compliment she felt was warranted. I'd been teasing her for the last few months that she might try saying "Thank you" one of these days.

"What you really need," I said, "is a special piece of jewelry to top it off."

I felt bad a second later, when she looked at me expectantly, perhaps thinking I'd brought her a gift. I quickly added, "How about Tinkerbelle?"

I caught just a half-second of disappointment in her eyes before she laughed. "Oh, you're hilarious!" she exclaimed as she rolled her eyes at me.

"What?" I asked. "Don't you remember how you thought it would be the perfect addition to my eighth grade dance ensemble?" I playfully punched her in the arm. "You don't want to wear it?"

Mia laughed. "Yeah, I remember I thought that was the most beautiful necklace in the whole world. I couldn't believe you didn't want to wear it!"

"I know. I was mean to you, too. I still feel bad about that. But that night was the first time I ever felt really pretty and fancy. I was just so nervous about it. What can I say? I'm sorry I was mean to my baby sister. Next time you offer the lovely Tinkerbelle necklace, I will wear it!"

We both laughed, and then Mia exclaimed, "Fat chance! It's mine! Mine, I tell you!" She topped off her statement with her best evil laugh for good measure.

I plopped down on the bed as Mia twirled from her bedside mirror to the bathroom. After a second, she peeked her head out of the doorway and said seriously, "Besides Kate. You've always been beautiful. You don't need Tinkerbelle for that." Then she pulled her head back into the doorway and started her makeup.

I continued to lie on the bed, truly touched at my teenage sister's sweetness, but feeling too awkward to tell her so at the moment. Still, I felt so proud of her that night. I remember realizing that she wasn't a little girl any longer.

As I woke up from the dream, my amazement grew. I had completely forgotten that whole encounter. What a gift our memories can be, I thought.

**Kara** is fourteen now, the same age I was when Mia tried to give me her Tinkerbelle necklace for the dance. Our son Michael and Lisa's daughter Mia are almost five years old, and of course are into everything. Brett and Mitchell are close friends and often golf together, whereas Lisa and I become more like sisters every day.

This weekend Mom and her long-time gentleman friend Malcolm are getting married. The reception is at Lisa and Mitch's estate. Mom didn't want a big ceremony, but she asked Lisa, Kara, and me to stand up with her. Little Mia is a flower girl, and Michael is a ring bearer. Robert and his family will fly in for the ceremony, of course. Mom has asked me to hold a picture of my sister Mia during the ceremony, so that she will be with us, too. I know I'll cry a bucket of tears, but they'll be tears of joy.

I feel confident that I've gotten away with killing Mortenson now. I know there is no statute of limitations on murder, but so much time has elapsed that I don't worry about it any longer. I just don't think about it every day, the way I used to.

Once in awhile, though, the murder I committed threatens to show itself like an iceberg's tip at the water's surface, reminding me of the importance of steering away from that sharp tip of truth. The truth, which I feel safe to speak about in every other aspect of my life, becomes my enemy then.

I feel it daring me to speak it, to brag about what I did. Brett would understand, I think. Or Lisa. But I push the secret back down below the surface, and the moment passes.

Or did, until last year.

Lisa and I had been shopping all day. After leaving the mall, I started driving south, looking for an art gallery that Lisa had read about in the area. We ended up on the freeway just outside of Belmont. It had been a good day without men or kids, and we were acting like the teenagers we once were. The radio was blasting, and I felt happy and free.

Suddenly, Lisa said something strange. "Let's see if we can find Mortenson's old place in Belmont and drive by it." She looked at me tentatively, obviously not wanting to upset me.

"Okay," I said, not the least bit upset. "But why?"

Lisa smiled. "I want to see where the bastard died." I could tell that it didn't enter her head that this might be considered a shocking thing to say. That was just classic Lisa.

I don't know why I acted as I did next. Maybe it was Lisa's bold statement. Maybe I felt so young and free that I felt immune from responsibility and consequences. Maybe the glass of wine I'd had at lunch affected my judgment. Or maybe I just needed to open the box that held my deepest secret, just a little bit, for my best friend.

I revved the car and sped toward Mortenson's place. I drove straight there, never hesitating. I stopped across the street and pointed to the place I last saw Mortenson lying dead on the pavement.

"There. That's where he died."

I'd purposely avoided looking at Lisa as I drove straight to the destination. I looked at her now, ready for the questions I saw in her eyes.

"Kate, you drove straight here."

"Yes."

"Have you been here before?"

"Yes."

"When?"

Instead of answering, I looked up at the sky. The powder-puff clouds moved slowly across a beautiful blue.

"Lisa, don't you wish we could do this every day? Don't you wish that life was just all fun and shopping with friends, and no pain and no death and no hard times?"

I looked back over at Lisa, who was looking at me with complete bewilderment. Instead of waiting for her answer, I went on.

"But it's not. Bad things happen. And when they do,

we have to handle it. We can either run away, or bury our heads in the sand, or we can face it, and handle it."

I looked steadily at Lisa, whose bewilderment had turned to a curious suspicion.

"Kate. Do you know anything about how Mortenson died?" I recognized her look of love and acceptance. It seemed to say to me, "Trust me. Tell me."

I smiled and opened my mouth, but didn't speak.

I looked down at my lap, and finally answered. "Of course. It was all over the news."

Lisa reached out and grasped my hand in hers. "No. I mean, did you have anything to do with his death?" Her eyes implored me to be honest. "Katie, did you kill him?"

I looked at Lisa. I loved her with all my heart. She knew things about me that I'd never even told Brett. I knew that if I was honest with her, she would never intentionally tell anyone. But... I couldn't bring myself to say the words. I had been too careful for too long.

"Lisa, he's dead. I wish I could take the credit for killing him, but I can't." I paused. "You wanted to see where he died, and we have. Are you ready to go?" This last statement came out abruptly, and I realized I was feeling miffed. Not with Lisa, but with myself. But she didn't know that.

"Kate, I'm so sorry. You're the sweetest, most wonderful person I know. I can't believe I asked you that! I've seen too much TV or something. Can you forgive me?" Lisa reached over and engulfed me in a hug.

"There's nothing to forgive, Lisa. And I'm not that nice."

"Okay, Katie. Let's get out of here."

As I pulled back onto the freeway, Lisa stared out the window. Neither of us spoke for several minutes. Then, without turning to look at me, Lisa said one last thing.

"Katie. Don't say anything. But I want you to know that I'd have done the same exact thing. And you're still the best person I know." With that, she turned to me and wordlessly zipped her finger across her lips and made a motion that she was throwing that invisible key holding my secret out the window. Then she reached over, turned up the radio, and asked me if I was interested in seeing the new movie at the Crest Theater sometime that week.

To this day, we've never spoken of it. I know I should regret letting Lisa guess the truth, but I don't. I didn't realize it until I heard her words, but I badly needed to hear someone tell me I'm still a good person.

I have to admit that everything that's happened has changed me. Today I'm more conscious than ever of the ripple effect of all of our actions, and the responsibility that puts on us to make good choices. Killing Mortenson certainly guaranteed that he could never hurt anyone again. But it also guaranteed that he could never help anyone again. It did, as his mother said, take away all his chances, for both good and bad future actions.

Just as Mia's were taken away.

When Mia died, I wasn't sure I could ever be happy again. But I am. Of course, I still have days when I feel a little blue. Gone with the Wind still makes me cry. But I have a wonderful marriage and two healthy, happy children. I have a wonderful best-friend and surrogate sister who can always make me laugh. And I have my sister in heaven Mia, who I know is the brightest star shining down on me.

I try my best to live a good life. I'm conscious of my choices, and I think I'm a pretty good person. Raising my children well is first and foremost, and I think that Brett and I are doing a good job with that. We're all happy, which counts for a lot.

It turns out that in the long run, I was right. Although I don't want to give Gary Mortenson too much credit for my life now, the naked truth is that a part of my happiness is tied to his death. Killing him healed me in a way that nothing else could have. And I haven't just healed, I've thrived. I don't think I could have done that if he was still out there walking around.

I've also learned something very important about myself. I can do anything I need to – anything – to protect my family. I'm brave! I hope I never have to kill anyone again. I really do. But if evil comes for my family again, I'll do what I have to in order to protect them. My biggest regret is that I didn't see Gary Mortenson coming. I couldn't save Mia. But I know now that I don't have to be afraid of evil. If some evil bastard comes near my family, he'd better be afraid of me.

The bottom line is that the only thing that really matters is the people you love. The bottom line is that I'm still happy, and living a good life with those people.

Meanwhile, Gary Mortenson is still dead, and the young women in the world are exactly one-less-monster safer.

And as for me, every night when I climb into bed, I thank God again for the blessings in my life, and the forgiveness of my sins. And then I curl into my husband's loving arms, and sleep like a baby.

# ACKNOWLEDGEMENTS:

Thank you to my family for all the love and encouragement. It really helped!

Thank you to Kristen Morris of Tigress Publishing for her expertise and for her patience in walking a first-time novelist through this process. I continue to be impressed with not just your knowledge and professionalism, but also by your passion for your work.

Thank you to Editor Amelia Boldaji for your insight. You are so gifted!

Thank you to Steve Montiglio for his amazing art and design. I'm simply amazed by your talent!

**Kelley Theron** is a pen name for the author, who is currently employed as a Detective investigating Sexual Assaults and Child Abuse for a large U.S. city police department.

Although *A Patient Enemy* is a work of fiction, it was inspired in part by the many cases investigated by the author.

The author chose to keep her true name a secret in order to avoid any fuss or distractions during her future investigations, and to avoid any discomfort for the victims of these crimes.

When not investigating crime, the author enjoys exercising outdoors and hanging out with her husband and kids. Her idea of heaven is a comfortable chair, a big mug of tea, and a good book.